skins

the novel

skins
the novel

ALI CRONIN

Text copyright © Hodder and Stoughton Ltd 2010
Characters copyright © Company Pictures Ltd/Stormdog Ltd 2010

First published in Great Britain in 2010
by Hodder and Stoughton Ltd

1

A Catalogue record for this book is available from the British Library

ISBN: 978 1 444 90004 0

Typeset in Baskerville by Avon DataSet Ltd,
Bidford-on-Avon, Warwickshire

Printed and bound in Great Britain by
CPI Bookmarque Ltd, Croydon, Surrey

The paper and board used in this paperback by Hachette UK Limited
are natural reyclable products made from wood grown in
sustainable forests. The manufacturing processes conform to the
environmental regulations of the country of origin.

Hachette UK Limited
338 Euston Road, London NW1 3BH
An Hachette UK company
www.hachette.co.uk

With very special thanks to Emily Thomas

Prologue

7am, and beyond the grind of the street cleaner outside I could still hear them in her room. She was trying to muffle the noise, but there was no mistaking what they were doing. How could she do this to me?

It's not real. It can't be real.

I lay half on top of the sheets, one hand stroking my stomach. My whole body felt numb, frozen. If only I could feel this. I wanted to feel it.

I stopped with the stroking, pulled the sheet back over me and rolled on to my side. Stared out of my window at the early morning sky – just beginning to brighten. I felt sweat on the back of my neck – it was already too hot – and my head was throbbing. My happiness lay shrivelled and shuddering inside me. She didn't love me. She would never have done this to me if she loved me.

Then they stopped.

'Thank fuck for that.'

I scowled up at the ceiling, my lips parted to let out a silent incredulous gasp.

It felt like the end of the world; the worst thing that had

ever happened to me.

If I had imagined for one second that I could believe in love, I saw now that I'd been deluding myself. Because it all ends up the same, whether you love them or not.

Everyone betrays you, in the end.

AUGUST

Week One

Effy

Saturday 1 August

Venice

So she chose Venice. I can see why. It's like one huge Disney castle, but so much more unreal somehow. And, it's a good long way from Bristol, and Dad and all the shit back there. So, well played Mother. Anywhere that puts enough distance between me and everyone else. JJ and Cook and Freddie. The three fucking musketeers.

I'd started something and I couldn't go through with it.

And being surrounded by water – like a giant moat, cutting us off from the enemy. Mum and I have run away.

We've rented a small apartment away from the centre and the tourists. The people who own it have gone out of the city for the summer. It's in a four-sided building with a big courtyard in the middle. Amazing. So picturesque. Even the peeling pink walls, they remind me of strawberry milkshake. There's a balcony, too. Rusting blue metal. Excellent for sitting, watching, smoking. Seeing and being unseen.

My bedroom, however, is a freak show. Barbie everywhere. A single bed. Ticky-tack picture of Jesus and Mary topping off the virginal vibe. Naomi and Cook would piss themselves laughing if they could see me now, I thought, when I dumped my case on the bed and stared around me. There's no computer. I found an internet café within a few hours so I can keep in touch.

If I feel like it.

Mum was depressed as soon as we got here. So it was grey and pissing with rain, and humid and it stank but, God, all she thinks about is herself lately. Her own fucking problems. Which she created by the way. Maybe I should have been more sympathetic, considering all the shit I've stirred up the past few months, but Mum hasn't really noticed, or seemed to care about that either.

What about me?

'What's the matter with you?' I asked.

'Nothing. I don't know,' she said wearily. 'It's not really what I expected . . . Maybe it was a mistake to come here?'

'Maybe.' I closed my eyes, irritated.

Make an effort, Effy. You know what it's like to feel shit.

I opened the shutters wide. The rain had stopped. Brilliant sunshine made me blink. And smile. 'See?' I turned back to Mum. 'Transformed.'

A pathetic, weak smile. 'Yes. It helps.' She got her cigarettes out of her bag and lit up. 'So, what shall we do now?'

'I'm going to have a shower,' I said. 'Then I'm going out to explore. And find an internet café.'

'Oh, wait.' She handed me a brown envelope. 'This is from your dad.'

I tore it open. Counted five one-hundred euro notes.

'Spending money,' said Mum. 'That should be enough. If you need any more, come to me.'

'Right, thanks,' I said ungratefully.

It'll take more than poxy money.

'Well.' She sighed. 'I'll sort this place out and make it more homely.'

Homely? If it makes her happy I suppose.

As soon as I got outside I lit a fag, got my phone out and switched it on, waited for my signal to arrive and deleted the roaming text. Ten minutes later a message, from Pandora. Something about Thomas and her mum. Send her pictures. Yes, Panda.

It was mid-afternoon, and quiet. On the corner of the street, a few old men sat outside a café playing dominoes; a mangy dog sniffed the ground around their feet. An exhausted looking woman wearing a full-length apron was scrubbing the steps of the building next to ours. She stopped for a minute to rest and caught sight of me, standing with my phone. She looked me up and down with disapproval, maybe envy. This was her life every day, scratch, scratch, make it clean. She dipped her brush back in her bucket and carried on.

I lit another fag and moved towards a low wall opposite our apartment building. I sat smoking, just doing my thing of people-watching. Staring. Three boys, my age maybe, came round the corner of the street. One of them, the tall one with a hat on, looked like Freddie. Beautiful. Bit full of himself. He caught my eye.

'*Signorina* . . . *Ciao* . . . *Ciao*.' He whistled. The two with him started aping around, whistling, yelling stuff I couldn't understand, moving closer to me.

'You know what "Fuck off" means?' I asked the tall one when they'd calmed down. 'Fuck. Off.'

'Ooooh. *Inglese*.' He started coming over. 'Very nice. Is on holiday?'

'*Quoi?*' I blew a perfect smoke ring.

The three of them cracked up. I hummed inside my head and I stuck my legs out. My feet were on fire, it was so hot. My legs were bare. I looked down at them, and then up at the three boys. They'd stopped laughing. There was silence. My breathing started to speed up, but I wasn't going to let them smell fear. I flicked my fag on to the ground in front of me and we all just stared at each other.

'So,' I said eventually. 'Any time you want to piss off is fine with me.'

'Excuse me?' said the tall one. 'We are only being friendly. Maybe it is you that will "piss off" now.' He looked at his friends. 'You are being dressed like a whore,' he added, without turning back. 'A f-uck-ing whore.'

I wanted to puke. Throw up all over them. I wanted my dad, my mum. Freddie.

I'd started something I couldn't finish.

'*Eh, che fate?!*' shouted a voice – an older bloke coming towards me, that expensive look about him. Suit, T-shirt. Poncy Italian shoes. He looked sharply at the three morons and spouted a stream of angry Italian.

The tall one leapt in the air and howled like a wolf. I smirked. Cook. Just like Cook. The other two did the same and then they took off running.

'*Ciao bella*,' one of them called back nastily as they ran. 'English bitch!' And then they were round the corner. Gone.

Which left me with George fucking Clooney.

'*Sta bene*?' he asked. 'You are OK?' He shook his head. 'Take no notice of these boys.'

'I wasn't,' I said, not smiling. 'But thanks.'

I got up, not feeling like exploring any more, and made for the entrance to our building.

'Ah, you are living here?' he said. 'Me too.' He held out his hand. 'My name is Alfredo, but my friends call me Aldo.'

My hands stayed put. 'Effy.'

We did this weird awkward smiling thing.

'You should not smoke,' he said, looking at the pack of cigarettes in my hand. 'It is very bad for the skin.'

'Thanks for the advice,' I said politely and smiled my most charming smile. 'I'll bear that in mind.'

He pushed through the big wooden door and held it open for me. We were standing in the lobby, which smelled damp, like a cave. I looked at all the old pigeon holes for everyone who lived here.

I'd like a pigeon hole, I thought. I'd like to get in one and hide there, for ever.

'So . . .' said Aldo. He started climbing the stone staircase, half turned back to me. 'You are here with your parents?'

'My mum,' I said. 'We're here for a month.'

'Ah. You are renting the Tropeas' apartment? Well . . . we must all have a grappa together perhaps? Welcome drink!'

'Grappa?'

'An Italian digestif, Effy. It burns the soul.'

In spite of not wanting to, I grinned. 'Your English is pretty good.'

'Thank you. I spent a year studying in London. I have been waiting a long time for someone to tell me that. I don't get to practise it much these days.'

We got to the top of the second flight of stairs, and Aldo felt in his back pocket.

'Damn,' he said. 'I have left my keys at my mother's house.' He rubbed his forehead. 'I am locked out of my apartment.'

'Right.' I bit my lip and thought about it. 'Do you have your wallet on you?'

'Yes, but—'

'I need a credit card, that's all.' I watched his face, which was confused. 'To pick the lock?'

He stared, not getting it for a second, then smiled a fucking amazing smile. He wasn't bad-looking. I hadn't noticed before.

'Clever girl. Now, how, and more importantly *why* did you learn to do this?'

'Because I thought it might be a useful skill?' I said, looking pointedly at his locked front door.

'And so it has been proved,' said Aldo, handing me his wallet.

I ignored the many credit cards on offer, including the platinum Amex, and picked a flimsier laminated card. Membership card or something. I knelt on the floor and slid the card as far as it would go into the space just above the lock, tilted it so it was touching the door knob, then bent it

8

back the other way and leant on the door. Done. I got up and rubbed at my knees.

'Thank you so much for your help,' he said. 'Would you like to come in for a drink?'

'No,' I replied. 'Thanks.'

Why did I say that? Because my default answer is always No.

I waited for him to insist, but he didn't. 'Well, Effy,' he said, and held out his hand to grasp mine. It was warm and dry, his hand, not clammy. Big, strong. 'I am indebted to you.'

We smiled at each other.

Keep him there, I thought. Don't go. I took a lock of my hair in my fingers and stroked it slowly. I once read in some magazine that men hate it when women play with their hair. Bollocks to that.

'Well. See you then,' I said slowly. 'Another time.'

Without waiting for him to speak, I climbed past him, up to our apartment, timing it carefully. When I got to the top of our staircase I looked back.

But he was gone.

Naomi

Sunday 2 August

Ritzy's

The music was deafening. Cook's arm thrashed out and smacked me in the face.

'Oi! Clumsy bastard.' I thumped him on the ribcage.

He moved closer to me. Pressed his face way too bloody near mine. 'Ah, Princess. The Cookie Monster is just being friendly . . .' He stroked my cheek.

I pushed his hand off, but struggled with myself not to smile, just a bit. The thing about Cook is that he is bloody irresistible. I don't fancy him. I mean, I'm on the other bus now, as it were. He's totally fucking out of control. The opposite of me. But sometimes, yeah, I wouldn't mind being able to just do and say what the fuck I want. I'd die before I told him this, but I secretly envy Cook. In a sick kind of way, obviously.

'Cook.' I gave him the despairing older-sister look. 'Just calm the fuck down, would you?'

He laughed like a maniac. 'I don't do fucking calm, Naomi. You know that.' He planted a wet kiss on my nose. 'Sure I can't tempt you back on the cock train?'

I wiped off his drool. 'The cock train?'

'Well, maybe not.' Cook had his eyes trained on something behind me. I turned. Emily was standing there. Big eyes looking doubtful. 'Your fellow carpet muncher beckons.'

I reached out and took Em's hand, pulling her close to me. 'We'll overlook that remark,' I told him sternly. 'Just this once. And only—' I pinched a handful of his cheek '—because you're just a pussy underneath.'

Cook sniggered, his face sweating – from the heat, from the MDMA. 'Fair enough, Naomikins.' He took a swig of lager and waved the can at us. 'See yous later, lezzers.'

Emily wrinkled her nose. 'What did he want?' she asked, really trying not to sound bothered that Cook flirts with me. Well, in his own twisted way.

'Nothing, baby.' I put my arms around her, slid one hand under her top and stroked her spine. 'Come on, let's go and do something deviant somewhere.'

'Here?' Emily smiled, looking sweet and filthy at the same time.

'Here.' I held both her hands and pulled her back with me towards the toilets. She followed me through a mass of grinding silhouettes towards the Ladies. As we got to the door, I kissed her, really softly, then firmly found her tongue. Emily moaned and pushed her hips into me.

'I'm so happy right now,' she said pulling away temporarily. 'If I died tonight, it would be totally fucking OK.'

'Me too.' I kissed Emily on the forehead.

11

I saw Cook raising his can up at me from across the floor. A smutty smile on his face. 'Sweet,' he mouthed, and he winked.

I grabbed Emily's hand and pushed quickly through the door.

Monday 3 August

Naomi's bedroom

'What time is it?' I rolled over and pressed pause on the iPod in its dock. It felt like the middle of the night to me. Emily and I hadn't got home till 2am. We stayed awake not wanting the night to end. Our last night. But we fell asleep in front of the shopping channel, a bit stoned, a bit drunk. Happy.

But this morning I felt cranky to say the least.

'About half eight?' said Em. She was painting her toenails. On my bed.

'Emily! Can you do that in the bathroom or something? You're going to get fucking Purple Haze all over my quilt.'

'All right all right, Jesus.' She got up off the bed and hobbled towards the door. She turned to look at me when she got there. 'What's wrong with you this morning?'

'Nothing,' I said automatically. I was scowling, as is my wont. I'm not proud of it, but old habits die hard. 'It's just . . . early.' I levered myself up on one arm. 'I'm not good in the mornings.'

She wasn't falling for it. 'Right . . . But . . . I'm going to France this afternoon and you're suddenly acting like . . . Like everything about me is getting on your nerves,' she said. 'You want me to go, don't you?'

I rolled my eyes. 'Yeah. I can't wait to get shot of you so I can start having the time of my life over the next few weeks. I'm counting the fucking seconds till you're on that ferry.'

Shit, her eyes were getting that watery look. She's a sensitive flower. Strange because Emily Fitch is way tougher than I'll ever be. I'm all mouth and no trousers. I'm obviously the bloke in this relationship.

Yes, Naomi. Relationship.

'No . . . Em.' I held out my arm and beckoned her back. 'Sorry. Look, you know I'm going to miss you. Loads.'

Emily smiled and just like that, my mood dissolved. She's like an angel. An adorable red-haired angel. I wanted to hold on to her and never let her go.

'Come here,' I said.

I met her halfway and grabbed her T-shirt, pulled it over her head and chucked it somewhere. I stared at her perfect tits. Soft, gorgeous Emily.

'I love you, Emily,' I said, stroking her stomach. I kneeled down and kissed it. Smelled her. Emily stroked my hair and we just stayed like that for a few minutes. I didn't want to stop being with her. Ever.

'Naomi,' said Em eventually.

'What?' I got up and put my arms around her.

She rested her head on my shoulder and said, 'You're not going to do anything silly are you?'

'Like what?'

'Like, I dunno. Out of sight, out of mind.'

I held her tighter. 'As if.'

'Not even Cook . . . I know you—'

'Listen, Em.' I let go of her to look at her properly. 'What happened with me and Cook was one totally insane blip in my otherwise sane life. I was trying to pretend I was . . . Well, that I didn't like you.'

Emily's eyes were still kind of glistening.

'Love you. That I didn't love you. OK?'

She relaxed. Dimples restored to peachy-faced perfection. 'Good. Because I am serious about this. About us. It's not some fucking one-off for me.'

'Me neither,' I said, still not knowing *what* it was really. I mean, I know I love her. I can't imagine not holding and kissing, and fucking Emily. But the jury's out on whether I'm gay or straight.

'Anyway, you can talk,' I said, pushing her hair off her face. 'What about the great love affair that was you and JJ?'

'Naomi!' Emily pushed me back towards my bed. 'I explained about me and JJ. You know bloody well it was a pity shag. I'M GAY.'

'Sssh,' I said laughing. I pulled her back with me on to the bed. 'Do you want to say that a bit louder? I don't know if they heard it in the Australian outback.'

The sound of someone walking down the hall towards the bathroom stopped us. Kieran or Mum. Em rolled over on to her back. And we lay in silence, little fingers entwined.

Emily

Monday 3 August

Naomi's bedroom, later

'Naomi,' I whispered. I touched her neck with my fingertip. I slowly stroked her skin from under her ear to her smooth, pale shoulder.

'Naomi . . . wake up.'

Naomi made a grunting nose and wrinkled her nose. I smiled. I've been smiling a lot lately. I turned on to my back and looked up at the ceiling, then around her bedroom.

Naomi's room is wicked. It's much cooler than mine. Or rather the one I share with Katie. With its inane fucking footballers and boybands on the walls. Her My Little Ponies are still on the window-ledge, too, with all her horrible jewellery and leopardskin thongs hanging off them. I just let Katie take over because, well . . . that's what she does. And I never used to mind either. But now I've finally grown a pair and started standing up to her. And it doesn't seem like there's any turning back now.

I carried on looking, and smiling. I just couldn't believe my luck. Couldn't believe that the girl I loved loved me back. For a while I thought it would never happen. I've liked Naomi since middle school. She's passionate, and clever. Poised. And her eyes . . . like the snow queen. Some people think she's cold. Just because she doesn't make stupid, shallow smalltalk. Not like Katie, who opens her mouth and crap pours out. Naomi is sincere. If people think that means 'cold' then they're wrong.

They are so wrong.

I yawned loudly. Then felt Naomi's hand on my arm.

'Shit. What time is it?' she said sleepily. 'Do you have to go?'

I rolled over to face her. She was rubbing her eyes. Then she stopped and we just looked at each other. Slow smiles creeping over both of our faces.

'Hello beautiful,' I said. 'It's late and I'm hungry. What do you want for breakfast?'

'You,' said Naomi, pulling me towards her and kissing me, gently at first, then harder. I was tingling with pleasure. I took her hand and led it down to where I wanted it. She hesitated and then her fingers started to do their work.

Oh my God, this is fucking heaven, I thought. I am in heaven.

Two hours later we were in the café having breakfast. Naomi: rabbit-food muesli, me: a huge sausage and ketchup sandwich. Naomi was eyeing my food with a smirk on her face.

'What?'

She swallowed some sawdust and yoghurt. 'You,' she said. 'Like your sausages, don't you?'

I chewed and snorted, nearly spraying her with half-eaten food.

'Oh yeah,' I said when I'd recovered myself. 'I love sausage. You should try it Naomi . . . You have no idea what you're missing.'

16

'Oh, I think I do.' She stuck her tongue out and wiggled it at me.

An old bloke eating a full English looked over at us and frowned. He picked up his paper and held it pointedly in front of his face.

'Fuck you,' I mouthed at his *Daily Mail*. Naomi rolled her eyes and pushed away her rabbit food. Her face glum all of a sudden.

'What's up honey?' I said, wiping my mouth with a paper napkin.

Naomi pouted. 'You're getting on that ferry,' she said matter-of-factly. 'That's what's up.'

'You are going to miss me, aren't you, babe?' I said, sounding like a broken record. 'You'd better miss me.'

'Hmm . . . At first,' she said, straight-faced. 'Then I'll probably lose interest.'

'Naomi!' I squealed. 'Bitch.'

'How many fucking times do I have to tell you?' Naomi grinned. She looked so delicious. I wanted to take a bite out of her. My stomach was flipping over and over.

'It's such shit timing,' I said. 'And Mum's going to be a total pain in the arse.'

Naomi nodded. 'Oh yeah,' she said. 'Your oh-so liberal mum.'

'Yeah, well. We can't all have mothers like yours.'

'For which you should be truly thankful,' said Naomi, sighing. 'I know your mum needs time to get her head around it. Us. I mean, I needed to get my head around it for fuck's sake. I s'pose I can't blame her. Not completely.'

'She's a nightmare right now,' I said. 'We're just gonna

17

have to have sex in front of her. It's the only way it's going to sink in.'

'Now that would be a nightmare.' Naomi looked delighted. 'I'd rather have a threesome with Katie and Cook.'

'Ugh. Naomi! She's my sister, you dirty bitch.' I thought about it. 'Fuck, you don't fancy Katie too, do you?'

Naomi played poker face.

'Well, of course,' she said. 'I mean, you *are* identical, right?'

Naomi

Monday 3 August

At home, evening

After saying goodbye to Emily in the afternoon I drifted on a cloud of loved-up bliss for a bit, but by the evening I was right back in Moroseville. I had three weeks in which to kick my heels and obsess over what Emily was doing, who she was with. I thought about her mum, who'd be on full anti-gay offensive. And Katie, sly cow. Obviously she'd be casting her own evil spells. Emily seemed to think that Katie would lay off the total bitchery she's been practising over us lately. But I'm not so sure. I've taken her twin away from her. That's how she sees it. She can't stand me. Feeling's fucking mutual.

Mum and Kieran were eating in the kitchen when I

finally came downstairs after two hours of lying depressed on my bed, listening to a medley of loud, thrash metal tracks on my iPod.

Cheer up, Naomi, might never happen.

Mum looked up as I came in. Gave me one of her half-sympathetic, half-exasperated looks. 'Hello love,' she said. 'Feeling OK?'

I grunted and pulled back a chair. Kieran eyed me warily. He's never quite sure whether or not I'm going to grass him up over the unfortunate incident in the classroom last term, when he'd tried to snog me. At the time I was totally outraged of course, because it's fucking illegal for a start. But Kieran's OK. I never thought I'd say this, but he makes her happy. And, indirectly, that has meant that all those sad losers who used to occupy our house like it was some kind of bloody commune have finally got the fuck out of here.

'Sit down then. Have some food,' said Mum. 'Emily get off all right?'

A vision of Emily and me in my bed earlier popped into my head. I couldn't help a small smile creeping over my face.

'Yes. Emily got off all right.' I inspected the casserole in front of me, but decided against it. 'Now I need to get a holiday job; I can't just sit around here all day.'

Mum swapped worried looks with Kieran. They obviously didn't want me hanging around the house either. Not judging by the amount of time they were spending in Mum's bedroom anyway. Bit of a buzz kill, having Naomi No Mates staring sadly into space.

See, this is precisely what I totally fucking hate about relationships. Attachment. You don't belong to yourself any more. You're sharing with someone else. So when they're not there, a part of you fades out with them.

But I've got what I wanted, haven't I?

'Well,' said Mum brightly. 'A job might take your mind off Emily. Better than moping?'

'Maybe I don't want to take my mind off Emily,' I snarled. 'You just want me out of the way.'

'Now, Naomi, that's not true,' said Kieran, looking well panicked at the thought of a row.

'Isn't it?'

'Oh grow up.' Mum started stacking up bowls and plates. 'Come on Naomi, this isn't like you. You're normally so level-headed.'

'Sick of that,' I said. 'Living in a doss-house for the past couple of years. Putting up with your fucking do-gooding. Being "level-headed". What about me acting like *I* want for a change? If you don't like it, tough.'

Silence. Kieran gazed desperately up at the ceiling. Poor sod.

'I think it's time we all went to bed,' Mum said calmly. 'Talk about this in the morning.'

It was 9pm. 'Yeah, that's right. You go back to bed,' I said. 'You must be knackered, after all.'

Mum ignored me, while Kieran shuffled out of the room.

I watched her loading the dishwater, wondering if I might have gone a bit over the top. Not that I was going to apologise.

Finally Mum switched the kitchen light off, pretending

she couldn't see my eyes boring into her. As she passed my chair she stopped and bent down level with my chin.

'Don't be so angry, Naomi,' she whispered. 'It's only love.'

Pandora

Tuesday 4 August

At home

Since my favourite day in the whole world, the day of the Love Ball, me and Thomas have been like peas in a pod. I was just so bloody glad he still loved me. I thought I'd really gone and fucked that right up. And I know I told Katie and Emily I never wanted to do sex again after Cookie, 'cause it just makes everythin' so weird, but I didn't mean it. I wanted to surf 'n' turf Tom like you wouldn't believe.

'Course, keeping my mum totally unaware of me becoming a woman at last is hard. Mum seems to know everythin' that's going on with me. I always walk to the end of our road to phone Thomas. She don't like me being around boys. What the flipping heck would she say if she knew what goes through my head these days!

If Effy hadn't gone off for the summer with her mum I could have talked to her about my feelings and stuff. She

22

knows all about boys. She should do, she's got half of them with their tongues hanging out for her. Boys ain't never been a problem for Effy. Least, up until she went and fucked Freddie. Effy went a bit weird after that, and I went a bit weird with Eff. She hit Katie with a rock. That ain't nice. I was proper cross with her after that. I'll always love Effy though. That won't never change. But I've got to make it on my own.

I called my lovely boy from the bus stop.

'Hi Thommo, it's Panda. Wanna come over Brandon Hill and do kissing?'

'I can't, Panda. I have to go to work. It is not the holidays for me you know?'

'Bunk off, Thomas . . . Go on. We can go see Auntie Lizzie and have tea. It'll be ripper.'

'Pandora, no. I have to pay my rent.'

I sighed. Poor Thomas. He didn't go to school because he had to pay for all this stuff for him and his mum and his brother and sister. He had to work like all the time. It weren't fair, because it meant I couldn't get the chance to jump him. Thomas said we didn't need to do that yet. He wanted it all to be perfect and romantic and stuff. I just wanted us to get started and do it. Proper. Thomas is my only ever boyfriend. Not like Cookie, who never wanted to know me when he weren't putting his thing in me. Thomas loves me. And I love him. I didn't want to ever think about what me and Cookie did. It made me feel ashamed.

'OK, Thomas. You win. Meet you at the bus stop on Granger Road after work then?'

'*Oui*, Panda. I will look forward to it very much,' said

23

Thomas. I could see his smile over the phone. '*Je t'aime.*'

'*Je t'aime aussi.*'

Walking back home I made a plan. First off, Mum and me needed to get real about stuff. I knew I couldn't keep it in for ever. Sexy thoughts. I still want to make cupcakes in my pyjamas and I don't think I look right in clothes like Katie wears. I'll never be sex on legs. But I do want sex. And I want it with Thomas. I want it more than anything.

I was gonna have to tell Mum about Thommo. Once she knows him, I thought, she'll love him too. It's just . . . she weren't gonna like it that I've got a 'boy' friend. Not to mention a boyfriend.

Mum was doing her meditating when I went into our living room. I sat down on the settee. I stared her out.

'Mum,' I said. 'Mum, I need to tell you somethin'.'

'Hmm.' Mum frowned. 'Panda Poo. I'm meditating.'

'I know but . . . Mum. I really need to tell you somethin'.'

Mum sighed. 'What is it Pandora?'

I waited a beat. I had to say it now, or I'd get chicken and never do it.

'You know . . . You know I've not ever had a boyfriend?'

Mum's dreamy face turned into a sucking-lemon face. Her eyes went all mean-looking and narrow.

'Of course you haven't, Pandora. Boys are for later. Much later. When you're grown up.'

I frowned. 'See. That's just it, Mum. I am kind of, sort of grown up now.'

Mum laughed and it annoyed me.

'It's not funny, Mum. You don't take me seriously. I'm not

24

little any more. Look—' I lifted up my blouse and showed her my 36C bra. 'My tits are flipping enormous.'

Mum's mouth opened in a perfect circle shape. 'Pandora! Pull down your blouse! Don't ever do that again. Ever.' She got up and started rolling up her yoga mat really quickly. 'Now, I suggest we go and have a cup of tea and forget that ever happened.' She took my hand and led me through to the kitchen. She put the kettle on while I sat down at the table.

It had all gone well wrong. I should have thought it through better. I'm so useless at standing up for myself.

'Now, Pandora,' said Mum. 'Earl Grey? Or how about some chocolate milk?'

Thomas

Tuesday 4 August

On the way to meet Panda

After work I went to Mr Sharma's shop to buy Panda a doughnut. He was leaning on the counter reading a newspaper and picking his nose. The noise of the door made him jump. I pretended to be searching for something in my pocket and when I looked up, he was tidying the cigarettes.

'All right, Thomas?' he said.

'Very well thank you, Mr Sharma. And you?'

'Enjoying the weather, anyway. The usual?'

I nodded. Mr Sharma is a true pessimist. To him the good

25

things are merely small consolation for a horrible life.

'Where's Pandora today?' he asked, putting a butterscotch and custard doughnut into a paper bag.

'I am on my way to meet her.'

'I bet you are. You're a lucky fucker, aren't you?'

'Yes I am,' I couldn't help smiling.

'Well don't do anything I wouldn't do.'

I ignored that. Mr Sharma in the throes of passion was not an image I wanted anywhere near my mind's eye. Even he assumed that Pandora and I were having a sexual relationship. All our friends assumed Panda and I were having a sexual relationship. I think the only people who didn't assume that we were at it *comme les lapins* as you say over here were my mother and Pandora's mother, and I do not think even they were convinced.

It is not that I didn't want to have sex with Pandora. I just wanted it to be *parfait*. I was not interested in doing it just anywhere like an animal. That way is for the likes of Cook. Not for myself.

I walked to meet Pandora with renewed conviction. This girl that I love deserves something better than a quick fuck behind a bench.

But as I approached our meeting point at the bus stop I could see Panda walking up and down like a crazy person. I quickened my pace.

'Hello Panda.' I grinned at my girl, but I could not raise a smile from her face. She was very upset. 'What has happened?'

'It's no good, Thomas,' Pandora said, wiping tears from her cheeks. 'It's no fucking good.'

'What has happened?' I sat down on a seat in the shelter and beckoned to Pandora to sit next to me. 'Have you had an argument with your mother?'

'Not really,' Panda sniffed. 'Well, kind of. I mean . . .' She shut her eyes. 'She don't listen to me. I tried to tell her about you. About how I'm grown up now. Old enough to have a boyfriend and, do stuff with him. You know?'

'Pandora! You talked to your mother about sex?'

'I wanted to.' Pandora held my hand. 'But I never even got that far.'

'Thank goodness for that.' I breathed out loudly. 'It is not respectful to talk about such things with your mother. She does not want to know about it.'

'Well, she should!' shouted Pandora. She let go of my hand. 'It's about time, Thomas. I'm ready.'

I looked down at the doughnut in its bag. 'The thing is, Pandora, I don't know if I am ready for that yet. Not with you. You are special. I don't want to blow it.'

'You don't love me, then?' Pandora looked terrible. She removed her hand. 'You can't love me.'

'No. It is precisely because I do that I don't want to rush to do this,' I answered her. 'We have time, Panda. The time will be right soon.'

Effy

Wednesday 5 August

A café in Venice

Fuck it's hot here. I finally took my boots off and put on flipflops yesterday. Some green Havaianas Mum bought me for a stupid amount of money. I felt naked in them at first. My boots and I have been through a lot of shit together. Like, they're my armour.

I got up really early this morning. I just couldn't face sitting at that table with its weird plastic top eating disgusting hard Italian bread and jam, with Mum putting on the fake happy act, trying to think of things for us to do together. She must have read that fucking *Time Out Guide to Venice* back to front, and now she wants us to go on a culture tour together. Make sure that no part of Venice is left unturned.

She's trying, I know she is, but everything about her gets on my nerves.

Since our first day, I was hoping I'd bump into Aldo again. I'd even go extra slowly past his floor and stop in the stairwell, listening for his door to open. I didn't have the balls to actually knock on it.

But this morning we collided by the pigeon holes. He was sorting through his post. My flipflops were making even more of a racket than my boots as I stepped down towards him. I don't do embarrassed, but I came close then. Aldo looked up at me and smiled.

'Good morning,' he said. 'How are you and your mother settling in?'

'Good thanks.' I looked at the mail in his hand. 'You've got a lot of letters.'

Aldo sighed. 'Yes, yes. Always bills to pay, money for my wife's lawyers. Money for my children ... And this apartment. It never ends.'

My wife. Who'd fucked someone else? I wondered. Him, or her?

'You've got kids?' I asked innocently, playing for time. 'You don't live with them?'

'I am getting divorced from their mother,' Aldo said. 'It is necessary to be apart from them. Though I don't want to be. It's hard.' He waved a brown envelope at me. 'And it is very expensive!'

'Sorry,' I said. 'It must be a bit shit.'

Aldo shrugged and stuffed the letters in his jacket pocket. He gave me a sidelong look.

'And where is your father?' he said straightforwardly.

'I have no idea.' My turn to shrug. 'They're separated.'

'I'm sorry. Poor you,' he said. 'It's hardest on children.'

29

We fell silent. Nice bloke I thought. Kind, but not too nosey.

'So, Effy,' he said after a bit. 'What are you doing today?'

'Dunno. Maybe explore some more,' I said. 'And get lost, probably.'

'It is a labyrinthine city, there is definitely a risk of that if you don't know it.' He paused. 'But sometimes it can be . . . liberating to be lost.' He looked straight into my eyes as he spoke. 'Don't you think?'

Come with me.

'Maybe you could come . . . show me around?'

He looked at his watch and then, just then, I saw his eyes flicker over my body. He paused.

'Why not?' he said. 'It will do me good, too.' He gestured me through the door first. 'Let's go.'

'Where are we going?' I asked.

'Santa Maria dei Miracoli,' he said, rolling the words on his tongue.

I imagined that tongue on other places. My tits for starters.

'And that is?'

'A church.'

'Great.'

'You'll love it,' he said.

'I'm an atheist,' I said.

He shook his head, frowning a little. 'Come on. You are surely more intelligent than that.'

Jesus. I seemed to have turned into Katie Fitch. The queen of thick and shallow.

'It was a joke,' I said feebly. 'Sort of.'

Aldo smiled encouragingly at me.

'Ah. The English sense of humour! I need time to adapt I think.'

We walked through a maze of cobbled streets and alleys where, up above, washing dried on balcony rails, and we shooed away all the half-starved cats to arrive in a small, scruffy square. A bell was tolling loudly.

'Here,' said Aldo, pointing at a weird flat-fronted building. 'The most beautiful place in Venice.'

It looked like nothing to me. Not like the church Dad used to drag me and my brother Tony to every Sunday when we were kids. Back when Dad fancied himself as 'spiritual'. Total bollocks obviously. That church had been big, gothic, imposing. This one looked like nothing from the outside.

Aldo sensed I wasn't exactly bowled over. 'Just you wait,' he whispered, smiling like he was about to share some amazing secret.

I felt a jolt as he took my hand and led me quietly through the huge wooden doors inside and across centuries-old marble flagstones, and then I could see his point. The walls were literally *covered* with brown and ivory marble patterns, leading up to a crazily high, carved wooden ceiling. It was Awesome. I could have immersed myself in it even more if I hadn't been so conscious of Aldo's hand on my back, right between my shoulder blades.

'Well?' he said. 'What do you think?'

'I think it's fucking amazing,' I whispered.

Aldo leaned closer and whispered back in my ear, 'Your

31

use of language is somewhat inappropriate, Effy, but your heart is in the right place.'

'Thank you,' I said, strangely thrilled.

He was wrong, though. My heart was really not in the right place.

Cook

Thursday 6 August

A bus stop

'Fuck me.' I took the spliff out of my mouth and gave it to Freddie. 'Fucking weak as piss, that. Who give you that, man? It's rancid.'

Freddie give me one of his little-boy-lost faces. Shrugged his skater-twat shoulders. 'Dunno. Mate of Karen's, I think.' He checked my face, which was full-on fucking incredulous. 'No, not Johnny White. I'm not fucking stupid.' He chucked the spliff in the gutter.

'Good to hear it, my friend!' I slapped his arm, pulled my hand away and wrung it in the air. 'You been fucking lifting forklift trucks, Fredster? Your biceps: hard as a fucking brick.'

JJ smiled, that serene smile. Don't drink, don't really smoke, our resident fucking looney tunes. What the fuck does he use to take the edge off? He pointed at the soggy spliff. 'Are you keen to get hassled by those two upset-looking policemen coming towards us? Or are you both off your heads? Literally, or otherwise.' He bent down, picked up the joint and threw it over his shoulder.

'Little bastard,' came this spindly old bag's voice behind us. 'Went straight in my shopping that did.'

Freds, JJ and I shrugged simultaneously. Fred and I smirked. Didn't know her. Didn't care.

'No respect for anything these days, you lot,' the hag went on. She poked JJ in the back. 'You, young man. I know your mother . . . she collects my library books for me. Oh, I've seen you in her car. Don't think I won't tell her what you've been up to . . .'

'I didn't. I wasn't—' spluttered JJ, red as a fucking beetroot. Freds and I snorted with laughter. And I couldn't help myself, I turned round.

'Fancy a quick one?' I said, running my tongue over my lips. 'Bus won't be here for ages.'

As the old crone opened and shut her wizened old trap, the three musketeers legged it all the way back to Fred's place.

I had a proposition for him.

Freddie

The shed

'Right Freds,' said Cook, rubbing his hands together like a dirty old man. 'I've got an offer you can't refuse.' Didn't like the sound of that, not least because he was probably right. Cook has a way of getting what he wants.

'You're gonna love this one. A little game to pass the time, just you and me.'

'What about JJ?' I said.

'Jay's already in the loop, right, Jaykins?' Cook leant forward in what he liked to call 'his' chair – it was in my shed but whatever – and pointed his fag at me.

'You pulled last night, yeah?'

'Yeah. So?'

'It was good, yes?'

'Yes, it was most enjoyable. Is this going anywhere?'

'Right, so: four weeks, you and me, whoever gets the most pussy wins. There's got to be deep penetration, man, and stuffing the same bird twice doesn't count.'

'Nice,' I said sarcastically. But as Cook's ideas go it wasn't bad. It didn't involve anything illegal, for a start. And for various reasons I was totally in the mood for oblivion of the sexual variety. Fuck it.

'Yeah, all right then.'

'Correct answer, my friend. GayJay's keeping score, but we're gonna have to steal some evidence to give him – sticky knickers, a jizzy condom . . . that sort of thing.'

'That doesn't sound sordid at all,' I said dryly.

It didn't really matter to me, though. Like I said, I've had it with the meaningful shit. I loved a girl. She fucked off and left me. I'm not falling into that trap again.

I still checked my phone every hour, though.

What was she doing now?

'So.' Cook stuck his hand out. 'May the best man win.'

I narrowed my eyes at him. So, that's your game is it? I thought. Well fuck it, then.

'Absolutely,' I said, ignoring his hand. 'Game on.'

JJ

Kebab shop

'Fuck off, fruitnut,' said Cook. 'This ain't got nothing to do with Effy. So, are you going to keep score?'

It was 2am and Cook and I were at the counter of Abrakebabra. We'd been at the Caves, where Freds and Cook had both had sex (not with each other. Even Cook draws the line somewhere. And not literally in the club, which I believe is frowned upon: Cook had it down an alley and Freddie left to go back to a girl's place). Pandora and Thomas and Naomi were there too, so it was a good night even if I did just dance on my own and try not to think about the fact that I was the only one without the option of post-club sex. I was sitting a song out drinking my fizzy water when Cook reappeared.

'I thought you were having sex?' I shouted.

'Yeah. Finished. Listen Jay, I've got a plan. Let's go.' And he dragged me to the kebab shop and bought me a chips in pitta.

He explained the rules, which nearly all made sense. In an entirely morally dubious way, obviously.

There's a reason why Cook came up with this game. I'm no fan of cod psychology and actually I'm rubbish at the empathy-slash-emotional-engagement side of things, but in this case even I could see it. Effy wanted Freddie the whole time she was with Cook: Cook lost that game. So he's invented one he thinks he can win, which he probably will as sexual intercourse to Cook is like Earth's yellow sun to Superman. Without it, he's powerless, or he thinks he is. (Which is of course where the Superman analogy breaks down as, unless you count pre-1986 incarnations, he really is powerless without solar energy, whereas I'm almost certain the blood would continue to pump around Cook's body even if he didn't have regular exposure to girls' naughty bits.)

I put my analysis to Cook. He wasn't impressed. Hence the fruitnut comment.

'OK, I'll keep score,' I said, finally. 'But, just out of interest, why didn't you ask me to take part in the game?'

Cook grinned in a childlike manner. 'Because you'd lose, Jaykins.'

'I believe it's the taking part that counts,' I said, frowning a little.

'And so it is. Which is another area where you may fall short, my virginal friend.'

'Get lost. I'm not a virgin.'

'Might as well be, mate.'

A fair point with which I couldn't argue.

All things considered, I was pleased Cook had come up with the game. It meant he and Freddie were friends again, that they'd be happy, and therefore that I'd be happy.

Relatively speaking, obviously.

Effy

Thursday 6 August

Venice by night

'So, Effy. What do you think of Vivaldi?'

Aldo and I were coming back from a walk. I was doing what Tony calls my unstable colt walk, swaying into him ever so slightly. He had both his hands in his pockets.

Whatever. He'd warm up eventually.

'Vivaldi,' I repeated slowly. '*Four Seasons*, right?'

'That's right,' he said. 'He was a Venetian. They put on concerts here all the time, but there's one tonight that I know will be excellent. Perhaps you would like to go. And your mother, of course?'

'I think she hates all that classical stuff,' I said. Which was true, luckily. 'But I'll give it a go.'

Fuck. Old churches, and Vivaldi. Even Pandora wouldn't believe this.

'Excellent,' said Aldo. 'It's his *Gloria*. A short choral work. Beautiful.'

We walked in silence for a bit, me feeling his presence like a fucking Ready Brek glow. In the lobby Aldo stopped to pick up the post he'd left behind earlier.

'Until this evening, Effy. I'll meet you at your apartment at seven.'

Mum looked bemused when I told her I was going to a concert with a middle-aged man.

'Tell me who he is again?' she said, squinting at me through her fag smoke.

'He lives in this block. I helped him get into his flat when he'd locked himself out,' I said. 'Look, it's just something to do. Nothing untoward.'

'Right. I wonder what interest he could possibly have in you?' she said, dry as a fucking bone.

'I don't know. Devil worship? Ask him when he picks me up.' I knew she wouldn't, thankfully.

When Aldo arrived I was just out of the shower so I shouted at Mum to let him in. I found them chatting at the kitchen table, each with a glass of wine. He drained his drink and stood up.

'It was a pleasure to meet you, Anthea,' he said. 'Are you sure I can't persuade you to join us?'

'I'm sure,' said Mum. 'Thanks anyway. Have fun.'

I followed Aldo down the hall, and looked back at her sitting at the table, guidebook open again.

Poor cow.

I didn't hold out much hope for the concert, and by the time it finished I wasn't listening. It was difficult with Aldo next to me, smelling of Dolce & Gabanna or Versace or whatever. His arm was touching mine. Just. But he never once looked anywhere else but ahead of him. Not even when I crossed and uncrossed my legs provocatively.

But at the beginning, when the orchestra played and the music built up and then the choir suddenly joined in and I could feel the sound echoing off the ceiling, well; it was weird. It was moving.

Remember Effy, I thought. Thou shalt not be moved.

'Wonderful,' said Aldo, as we walked out into the humidity. It was ten-thirty and twenty-eight degrees. He regarded me, a little smile on his lips. 'I hope you didn't hate every minute of it?'

'No, I . . . liked it,' I said. 'I enjoyed the experience.' It was true. I had enjoyed sitting next to him. I would have preferred it if he'd put his hand on my thigh and slid it between my legs, but older blokes are obviously less forward in coming forward.

'I'll settle for that,' Aldo said. 'Now. What would you like to do? A walk back to the apartments?'

'Fine.' I didn't want to go back, though. I was enjoying myself.

'We must think of something to do next time that your mother would enjoy,' Aldo mused as we walked slowly, up and down over little bridges.

Must we?

'Thing is, she's not very . . . sociable at the moment,' I said disloyally. 'Personal stuff stressing her out. You know.'

'Oh.' He glanced at me. 'I can empathise with that.'

Great.

'Very messy personal stuff,' I added. 'You don't want to go there.'

'I see. You are protective of her. I can tell. It must be difficult for both of you.'

'What is?'

'Well . . .' He looked awkward. 'That your father is not around.'

'I don't think it's difficult for her at all,' I said.

I could feel his eyes on me. 'And why would that be?'

'Because it's what she wanted. She always gets what she wants. And then it's a big fucking mess and she starts whining about it.' I looked across at him, calmly. 'I don't feel sorry for her at all.'

If Aldo was taken aback by my heartlessness he didn't show it. He took my arm as a couple nearly careered into us, and I found myself temporarily pulled into his chest. Felt the warmth coming from him. 'In my experience things are rarely that simple,' he said quietly. 'Perhaps it is worth trying to understand.'

Fuck that. I nearly laughed in his face. Instead I put my hand to my forehead and closed my eyes.

'Effy? Are you all right?'

'Just a bit dizzy,' I lied. 'It's the heat.'

He felt my cheek with the back of his hand. 'You are a little hot.' He shook his head. 'You English women. You are fragile creatures.'

Our eyes locked.

I held his gaze. Looked at his wide, soft mouth, tanned cheekbones, dark-lashed eyes.

I wish you'd kiss me.

Instead he took my arm and led me over bridge and down cobbled alley, back to our apartments.

I got back, and walked into the kitchen to find Mum at the table drinking Sambucca with a little old lady. 'This is Florence,' said Mum. 'She lives in the next-door apartment. Florence, this is my daughter, Effy.'

She looked ancient (the old lady, not Mum, although the last few months have taken their toll), her skin covered in wrinkles, but she was sitting bolt upright, her hand firm as she lifted her mug. She was rake thin, with bright white hair twisted and fastened at the nape of her neck. She was wearing a petrol blue shirt-dress with a triple strand of black beads that reached to where her cleavage would've been if she'd had any tits to speak of.

'Nice to meet you,' said Florence. English.

'You too,' I said. 'I like your beads.'

She reached up to touch them. 'Oh, thank you,' she said. 'They're lovely, aren't they? Genuine ebony, of course, which I suppose would be frowned upon now but I got them in the seventies. There's no substitute for the real thing, is there Effy?'

'Guess not,' I said. Fucking brilliant, we travel hundreds of miles to Italy and Mum manages to befriend a senile old English biddy.

'Florence moved here from London ten years ago,' said Mum.

'My husband was Italian but we always lived in Wimbledon,' said Florence. 'When he died I felt a tremendous urge to live in Italy. Perverse, really.'

'Yeah.'

'I decided on Venice because it was the place where we first made love. Second of September 1939, the day before war was declared. The ecstasy before the agony, so to speak. Benito was a stupendous lover. Beautiful fingers.'

OK, maybe I was going to like her.

'Do you have a lover?' Florence asked me, as I sat down at the table. Mum let out a faint ripple of laughter. I studied the old lady's face for a moment. Was she for real?

'Not really, Florence,' I said. 'Do you?'

Florence started laughing and ended up coughing, hacking up what sounded like decades of fag gunk. She thumped herself in the chest and said, 'Ha ha! Touché, Effy! Alas, those days are over for me. I'm afraid it's a case of the spirit isn't willing, and neither is the flesh. Nowadays I use Sudoku to get me off to sleep.'

'Good tip, Florence,' I said, unable to keep a genuine smile off my face. 'I'll give that a try when the time comes.'

That night sleep was a long time coming. I lay awake for hours, a hybrid of Aldo, Freddie and Cook invading my thoughts, and my body. I worked my fingers inside me. I wanted him everywhere.

I wanted to wake up next to him.

Emily

Friday 7 August

Bonjour France Vacances! Resort, nr Bordeaux, France

'Ooh, hello,' said Katie loudly, tossing her hair like a frisky Shetland pony. 'What do we have here?'

It was day four of our jolly family *vacances* but the first day here, at Butlins *de la Mer*. We'd stopped off at Cecile and Ed's (friends of Mum's and Dad's) place in Lyon for a couple of days and Katie and I had done a pretty good job of avoiding each other. Helped by the fact that Cecile's nineteen-year-old son Fabien had been shagging her in his bedroom most of the time. James isn't much better company, but at least I can hit him whenever he opens his mouth.

So now Katie and I were tolerating a rare moment of occupying the same proximity, sitting on the mound of decorative rocks outside our chalet, watching a family arriving, climbing the steps up to theirs. A fit boy with dark curly hair and long brown limbs was carrying a lilo and a huge rucksack. Katie leaned back on her arms, pushing her legs into a position where they looked longer and thinner than they actually are.

The boy carried on up the steps. He didn't seem to have heard her, didn't even glance at her. Bad luck, Katie.

'Hey,' she said sharply. 'Are you deaf and blind or something?'

He stopped, and looked down at her. 'What?'

'Forget it,' said Katie, getting up and brushing grit off her arse. 'Loser.' She clambered haughtily down the rocks to the beach.

'Charming.' He looked at me, did a double take, and raised his eyebrows. 'Jesus. There's two of you?'

I laughed for the first time in about four days. 'Ignore her,' I said, extending my hand. 'We are so not identical. My name's Emily.'

'Josh.' He was luscious, I'd give him that. Katie'd totally blown it with her fucking hissy fit. He looked back at her, striding angrily across the sand.

'Does your sister know she's got her mini skirt tucked into her thong?' he said.

I liked him already. 'Oh, she knows all right,' I said as my mother came out of our chalet, beaming like a hetero-seeking satellite. I stood up quickly. 'Better go, maybe see you later.' I skipped past Mum who was no doubt already planning her wedding outfit.

'Definitely,' said Josh. 'Later Emily.'

'So?' said Mum as we all sat down for our dinner. 'You've

45

made a new friend then, sweetheart?' Fair play to her, she'd managed to restrain herself for a whole hour while she was getting the food ready.

'What? Who?' I said, innocently. I ate a mouthful of lamb chop.

'The boy. Josh is it? He's very handsome.'

'Oh, him.' I reached across for the red wine to pour myself another glass. 'Yes Mum, he's really good-looking. I think Katie wants him, though. Right Katie?'

'No way,' Katie snarled, pushing her food round her plate. 'Pretty boys like that are not my type.'

Like fuck they aren't.

'Mine neither,' I said, looking pointedly at Mum. 'Obviously.'

Mum rolled her eyes and gave me a totally infuriating 'We'll see' smirk.

'Oh, you could do a lot worse,' she said. 'Both of you.' She started collecting up the plates and carried them over to the kitchen counter. 'Anyone for apple tart?'

Here we go.

'HELLO? I'm GAY,' I hissed loudly.

'Whatever you say, darling!' trilled Mum, doling out helpings of tart.

Jesus. I preferred Angry Denial. A whole two weeks of this shit.

'No dessert for me,' I said, grabbing my phone. 'I've got a call to make.'

I sashayed past Mum, who pursed her lips, desperate to have the last word.

'Yeah,' said Katie. 'None for me either. Got to watch

my fabulous figure.'

'Even if no one else is,' I quipped. I made quickly for the bedroom, slamming the door in Katie's face as she got there.

'Fucking muff-munching bitch,' she said, rattling the handle aggressively.

I let her in after five minutes of rattling and door-beating, and decided to call Naomi from somewhere more private. The beach would do. I left Katie trussing herself up like Jordan's little sister. False eyelashes, cement mix foundation, skirt up to her fanny. But what do I know. She'll no doubt find some moron to have sex with her. I didn't imagine they'd be that fussy down at 'Foam Nite' – the village disco organised by the holiday reps. I'd rather kill myself than attend that little gathering.

It was a clear night as I walked down to the beach. Sky turning darker and darker blue. The stars were starting to come out. I lay on the sand, looked up at them and thought about Naomi. I missed her like hell. I checked the time on my phone: not too late to call. She answered immediately.

'Hey lover.' It was so good to hear her voice I could have cried.

'Hey you. How's it going?' I said.

'Oh, you know. Amazing. Watching Mum and her boyfriend totally loved up really can't be underestimated as a form of awesome entertainment. I never knew just how stimulating it is watching two old desperados pawing each other every second of the fucking day.'

'Fuck, honey. That's evil.'

47

'Yeah. It's shit. But tonight was always going to be a bit shit.' She sighed. 'How about you?'

'Same. Going out of my mind. Mum's already tried to set me up with a boy.'

'Oh, Jesus. Who?'

'Just a kid who's got a chalet next door. Seems OK actually.'

Silence.

'Though, *obviously* I am not interested.'

'Whatever. Think I care?'

'I should fucking well hope so!'

I knew she was smiling, though she didn't answer.

'I wish you were here with me right now, on this beach, looking up at the stars,' I said.

Naomi groaned. 'Me too. I can't stop thinking about us in my bed.'

'I know.' I hesitated. 'Remind me . . . What were we doing in your bed?'

'Well . . .' Naomi began, but then I heard footsteps behind me.

'Fuck, someone's coming,' I hissed down the phone. 'I'll call you back.'

I turned around to have a go at whoever was creeping up on me. It was Josh.

'What are you, some kind of perv?' I said, looking up at him. I couldn't see much in the darkness, but I could tell that he was smirking.

'Um, no,' he said. 'I'm someone with ears. There's no breeze: sound travels.'

'Right.' I stared at him, clutching my phone.

'Right. Well. Sorry. I'll leave you to it,' he said. He trudged off up the beach.

I felt a bit bad.

'Hey?' I called after him. 'If you're not doing anything tomorrow . . . Maybe we could, you know, hang out or something?'

Josh grinned. 'Sure,' he said, walking backwards now. 'I'd like that. Just give us a knock.'

'Excellent.' I gave a cheery little wave.

I watched until I saw him go into his chalet then picked up my phone and pressed redial.

'Hey you,' I said. 'I was worried you might have gone to sleep.'

'No chance. Not when I'm thinking about undressing you.'

'Yeah?'

'You've got your white cotton knickers on, and I'm kissing you up the insides of your lovely thighs . . .'

'Should I take my knickers off?'

'No . . . I'm doing that. Then I'm going to move further up . . . Slowly at first then . . .'

'Faster,' I said breathlessly. 'Do it faster.'

'You love that,' she said.

'I fucking love it. Can you see my tits?'

'Yes, and you're touching them . . . your nipples are hard. And I'm rubbing myself up and down your thigh.'

'Jesus . . .' My heartbeat was skipping, increasing. I had my hand down inside my knickers, my fingers probing as I imagined they were Naomi's tongue. 'I'm going to come,' I said breathlessly. 'I want to kiss you—'

With a euphoric rush I came, one hand trembling clutching the phone to my ear.

'I love you,' I said, at the same time as Naomi. 'I love you so much.'

Katie

Friday 7 August

The beach, late

I climbed off the boy's increasingly limp dick.

'Fucking excellent shag, babe. You're hot,' he said, pulling the condom off and reaching down to pull his shorts up from round his ankles.

I brushed the sand off my clothes and got dressed. 'Yeah, brilliant. See you around.' I leant down, kissed him and, with a quick stroke of his balls to remember me by, walked away up the beach towards the marina. I had no intention of seeing him again, but it was good to leave on a high note.

The village Foam Nite was obviously fucking lame, but at least I'd pulled. To be honest I could take my pick. I was wearing my new lime green bodycon dress over leopard print bra and thong. And I'd had a Brazilian the day before we left Bristol. When I got to the club I went straight to the bar. Before I'd had a chance to order, someone was offering to buy me a drink, but I was way out of his league so I politely declined. Next one to come up to me was much more like it.

Tall, good looking, cheeky smile.

'Buy you a drink?' he shouted over the noise. I looked him up and down, took in the hint of sparkling white boxers above his jeans, the faded blue T-shirt, the mussed-up black hair, and smiled my cutest smile. 'Sure. I'll have a V 'n' T, thanks.' He grinned and leaned over me to order. He smelled nice.

'How come you're here on your own?' he said, handing me my drink. 'Where's your boyfriend?'

'I don't have a boyfriend,' I said. 'And I'm on my own because I didn't come here to dance around in foam.' I looked up at him batting my eyelashes.

'Naughty girl,' he said, stroking my arse.

Half an hour later, we were on the beach. He wasn't the most sensitive of lovers, but that's hardly the point any more. Sex is sex. And sex was the only thing getting me through this painfully lame holiday. That, and the thought of what I'd left behind. There was nothing in Bristol for me, unless you counted humiliation and painful memories. Which I didn't, funnily enough. Two weeks when I absolutely definitely could not bump into Freddie could only be a good thing, even if some of it was in a crappy resort that would basically be fucking Blackpool if it wasn't sunny all the time.

Sunbathing all day and fucking all night. I can think of worse ways to pass the time. I'd started as I meant to go on, shagging a posh boy from a stag party in an empty cabin on the ferry over here. He was pretty vile actually, keeping his rugby shirt on and bellowing, 'Oh God, yah,' when he came.

Then Fabien at Cecile and Ed's place. Bit of a nerd but he fancied me, which is always the aim, and he fucked me good in his bedroom for about eight hours. I'm sure his parents knew because of the noise. But no one said anything. Must be OK in France. They're more comfortable with sex. Actually it was painful after a bit, but I've got used to pain. Water off a duck's back. It's better than feeling nothing.

Emily doesn't approve of course, but she can fuck right off. She still can't stand it that I'm just more fuckable than her. Yeah, she's wandering around with that smug look on her face right now, like love's young dream has punched her in the face. But I've got news for her: it doesn't count if you're a lezzer. It's not the fucking same.

When I got in, Em was fast asleep. I sat on my bed and pulled off my clothes. My whole body felt sore actually. Bruised. I usually sleep naked but I nicked one of Emily's voluminous lesbo T-shirts, got into bed and tucked my knees into my chest.

And I tried not to cry.

Emily

Saturday 8 August

The chalet

It was gone 1am by the time I got to bed and God knew what time Katie got in, so neither of us were interested when Dad tried to wake us at half-eight. I tuned him out but caught the words 'family' and 'surfing lessons'. Enough to ensure I was comatose till noon. When I woke, Katie was gone and I had the house to myself. Bliss. I padded through to the kitchen in my PJs and made a cup of tea. I was spreading jam on baguette when Mum, Dad and James got back from their morning of water-sport-based bonding.

'Aha, she wakes!' said Dad. Still in jovial mood, then. Brilliant.

'I'm glad you're up and about,' said Mum, picking up the kettle to refill it. 'I thought you, Katie and I could spend the afternoon at the spa. Bit of girlie time. I said I'd meet Katie in town in a bit.'

I'd really, really, rather not.

'Thanks Mum, it's a nice thought, but I'm not really in the mood. I was going to go for a walk. On my own.'

'Oh come on, Emily. Snap out of it,' said Mum.

Fuck's SAKE.

'Snap out of what? I'm fine. I just fancy an afternoon to myself.'

Mum sighed. 'Fine. Maybe tomorrow then.'

'Yeah. Maybe.'

So she was still skirting round the elephant in the room. Fine by me if she didn't bring it up, but it made everything so fucking fake.

I didn't bother mentioning that I was planning to hang out with Josh today. I'd never hear the fucking end of it. I waited till everyone had finally left before I grabbed my stuff for the beach and stopped off at his chalet.

I knocked and the door opened pretty much immediately.

'Thank God for that,' said Josh. I could hear a woman's raised voice in the background as he pulled the door to behind him. I raised my eyebrows.

'My mum,' he said. 'She does go on, bless her. I would invite you in, but she's already wetting her knickers at the thought of a potential playmate for the deviant son.'

We started walking down the steps to the sand.

'So,' I pressed. 'Deviant?'

'Long story, Emily. Let's just say Mummy isn't the most progressive woman in the world.'

A little light went on. 'Ah-ha,' I said. 'You're gay.'

Josh brushed his hair back with exaggerated campness.

'Me, darling? Why ever would you think that?'

'Just a wild guess.'

'Good work, Sherlock.' He looked at me. 'And you?'

'Same,' I said. 'Is this when we do the high five to like, bond and shit?'

He grinned. 'Yeah, if we were a couple of jock wankers we would.' He looked me up and down. 'I thought there was something about you. My foolproof gaydar again.' He looked back at our chalet. 'Your parents are cool with it I assume?'

'Nope. They're pretending it isn't true. You know. Total denial, that sort of thing.'

We got to the bottom of the rocks. Josh took off his flipflops and stuffed them in his backpack. It was scorching. Not a single cloud anywhere. The beach was already filling up.

'Want to find somewhere more private?' said Josh. 'I heard there's a rocky little beach round the headland over there.'

'You mean that headland that looks about five miles away?' I groaned.

But half an hour later, we found ourselves on a deserted stretch of sand away from the screaming kids.

We lay our towels down by some rocks and I slathered myself with Factor 50. I stripped off to my tankini and sat down.

He sat down beside me and for the first time I could look at him properly. Longish curly brown hair, hazel eyes, broad shoulders, and wearing low-slung khaki swim shorts.

'Listen,' he said, as we stared out to the perfect sea and watched a couple of boats bobbing about on the horizon. 'I just wanted to apologise for embarrassing you last night, when you were on the phone.'

'Forget it. I'm sorry if I sounded arsey. I'm just a bit pissed off at being on holiday with my parents. Y'know, missing my girlfriend.'

Josh poked at some pebbles with a bit of driftwood.

'I know exactly what you mean. I broke up with my boyfriend a couple of months ago. It's why I'm here – my parents persuaded me to tag along 'cause they thought it'd cheer me up. And of course they hoped it would open my eyes to the fact that I'm actually deep down a red-blooded heterosexual.'

'Fuck, what are they like,' I groaned. 'Everyone in my family hates Naomi. That's my girlfriend. It's like *she* turned me gay. If only they knew it was me who pursued her . . .' I adjusted my sunnies. 'The worst one is Katie. My sister. She can't stand it that I'm not like her. She's a fucking magnet when it comes to blokes. She's full of herself, you know?'

'Actually she seems pretty insecure to me,' Josh said lightly.

'You are joking?' I said. 'Insecure?'

'Totally. She's desperate. That display yesterday when I arrived with Mum and Dad. Knee-deep in neediness.'

For some reason this bothered me.

'She's not needy!' I said. 'She's always been too fucking confident if anything. She's never without a boyfriend.'

'Of course she isn't. She probably gives it up to anyone.' Josh turned to face me. 'It's an act, Emily. I've met loads like her.'

'Right,' I said quietly. 'Maybe you're right.'

It was about time my sister and I had a proper chat.

Effy

Saturday 8 August

Venice

Mum, Florence and I got through three bottles of wine last night, and I still found myself raiding the cupboards in our apartment for more alcohol at midnight. I found a bottle of what looked like liquid lemon curd. I poured half a bottle into a mug. Fucking disgusting. I vomited for an hour and then fell asleep on the bathroom floor. Mum discovered me.

'Jesus.' She knelt down, took hold of my chin and gave my head a shake.

I opened my eyes. 'What?'

'Don't you know when to stop?' she said witheringly.

'Stop what?' As I spoke I could feel the dried sick on my mouth cracking.

She frowned.

'Half a pint of Limoncella on top of all that wine? Oh God . . . And you've vomited all over my make-up bag.'

She got up and rinsed out a flannel in the sink.

57

'What are you doing?'

'I'm going to wash this mess off. Christ, the state of you.'

Before I could protest she started gently wiping my face. It was nice. Soothing. For a few minutes there was just the sound of her bracelets clacking together and my breathing.

'Too late for a bath,' she muttered. 'No hot water, anyway.' She stopped with the flannel and stroked my hair back off my face. 'Come on. Time for bed.'

'Leave me alone.'

She ignored me.

'Let's get this off. And your skirt.'

She took hold of my arms and pulled me up to sit on the side of the tub.

'I can undress myself, Mother. I'm not a baby,' I said, just as an agonising ripple of pain shot through my skull. 'Just get me some fucking paracetamol. I'll be fine.'

'Don't move,' she said and went out into the hallway. Two minutes later she was back with something large and white she'd obviously nicked off an old lady.

'A nightdress? You've got to be fucking kidding me.'

I got unsteadily to my feet. I was naked and shivering badly. Mum slid the granny garment over my head, pushed my arms through and then buttoned it up to the throat. I felt about five.

'Good girl,' she said soothingly. 'Good girl.'

She took my hand and led me to my bedroom, pulled back the sheet on the bed. I collapsed back on the pillow.

'Mum,' I said drowsily, watching her close the shutters. 'Don't close them all the way.'

She left them and came towards me. Tucked the sheet

around me and turned the light off.

'You'll be OK, Effy,' she said. 'Everything's going to be fine.'

But at noon today we were back to the cold war. OK, I'd let her look after me, but I was under the influence. It didn't mean we were going to have a fucking bonding session this morning. All the stuff that was there before, it was still there.

I wandered into the kitchen feeling like shit. Mum was at the table with her back to me. I closed my eyes. My head reeled. I drank some orange juice, took three aspirin and picked up the spare set of keys.

'I'm going out.'

Mum looked up from the phrasebook she'd been studying, pointlessly as she hasn't spoken a fucking word of Italian since we got here. 'Where?'

'Just out to get some air. And I might go and see what's-her-name.'

'Florence?' said Mum. 'I might come with you.'

'In that case I'm going to the internet café,' I said calmly.

'What the hell is the matter with you?' Mum sat back angrily in her chair.

'I just want to be alone. Understand?' I was being a bitch, and she didn't deserve it. But I've got a reputation to maintain.

'You're not interested in joining us later then?' she said lightly, closing her book, and pouring herself more coffee.

'Us?'

'Aldo has invited me – us – on an excursion to a little island off Venice.' She said. 'Lido, I think it's called.'

'Right.' I fought the urge to kick her chair. 'Well, yeah. I'll come. Why not.'

Mum smiled and lit a cigarette. 'Good. I could do with some proper sea air. We've picked the hottest time of the year to come to a bloody city in the Mediterranean. No wonder the locals all bugger off to the country. Oh well . . .' She started putting stuff into her bag: sunglasses, wallet, phone. Make-up. 'He's a nice man, isn't he? Kind.'

And he's mine, I thought. Not yours.

There was a loud knock on our door.

Mum looked at her watch. 'Shit. I didn't realise it was this late. That must be Alfredo now.'

'I'll get it,' I said, darting out of the kitchen.

When I opened the door to our apartment, Aldo was standing there with Florence. Her arm linked through his.

'Hello dear.' She beamed at me. 'I hope you don't mind an old lady tagging along?'

I would have been pissed off if it had been anyone else. But Florence can charm the birds off the fucking trees. And she could keep Mum company.

This might work out OK in fact.

' 'Course not,' I said. 'The more the merrier.'

As we all trooped down the stairs, Mum leading the way, Aldo turned back to me. 'Lido is an extraordinary place, Effy,' he said. 'It is part of Venice, but very different. The architecture in particular. A lot of shabby art deco buildings that were once very grand. Now it is, I think you English would say, more of the faded glamour. And it is a little eerie. It is where *Death in Venice* was set?'

60

I looked blank.

'A film directed by Luchino Visconti. Very disturbing.'

'And a book,' Mother piped up. 'About a writer who falls in love with a young boy.'

I bet she'd only read that this morning in her beloved fucking guidebook.

But I was looking forward to it. Lido sounded like the kind of place where the real becomes unreal.

And that suited me down to the ground.

We took a water taxi over to the island, and the salty air slowly worked away my headache. As we sped away from Venice, I looked back at the city, smouldering in the heat.

Mum thought she was in the Dolce fucking Vita or something, with her headscarf and sunglasses. The wind whipping her hair around. I smirked at the back of her head.

When we arrived Aldo took us straight out for lunch at a posh hotel near the water. An amazing peach- and gold-coloured building where the staff looked like they'd been trapped in time. And behaved like it, too. I swear the bloke who showed us to our table actually bowed.

As soon as we sat down, I stood up again.

'Where are you going?' asked Mum.

'Loo,' I said, not looking at her. I needed to get myself together.

In the toilets I hauled myself up on one of the sinks and sat for a while, massaging in the free hand cream and staring at everyone who came in. They all looked away uncomfortably. Not my fault if they chose to be freaked out by me. I wasn't doing anything wrong.

'Ah, here you are!' said Aldo, smiling at me when I got back. 'I was wondering where you'd got to.'

'Just looking around,' I said, pouring myself a large glass of wine. 'Nice place.'

'Isn't it. I have only stayed here once, on my wedding night.'

'I'm surprised you can bear to come back,' said Mum.

'On the contrary, it is a very happy memory for me.'

I drained my glass and poured another large one.

Refloat the boat, as Dad would say.

'Effy, slow down,' said Mum.

I ignored her and took a huge gulp of wine. That was more like it. I was starting to feel good and pissed. I gestured to a waiter to bring the same again.

'Effy . . .' said Mum, as if she was warning a toddler to stay away from a power socket.

'Oh take it easy, Mother,' I said. 'Lighten up. Have some more wine.' I clumsily poured some into her glass, then Aldo's, Florence's and my own. I felt as though I was hovering above our table, looking through narrowed eyes at Aldo trying to make conversation with Mum as she ate her spaghetti Bolognese. How adventurous, Mother. Why didn't you just order egg and chips and be done with it.

Florence caught my eye and smiled knowingly.

A ripple of applause brought me back to earth. On the other side of the room some bloke in a white suit bowed then sat down at a grand piano, flicking the tails of his coat out as he did so. I laughed way too loudly and a couple of people frowned over at me. Fuck them.

He started playing that Billie Holiday song. 'Lover Man,

Oh Where Can You Be?' One of my favourites believe it or not. I leaned over, my hands in my lap, and looked into my glass, inhaling the sweet pungent smell and I hummed along.

'Lovely,' said Florence. 'Takes me back.'

I swivelled my eyes up to look at her. She met my gaze and smiled again, then subtly raised her glass.

'To awkward situations, eh Effy?' she half whispered.

I waved my own glass about precariously, wine sloshing out and over the table. Mum looked uneasy.

'What awkward situation?' she asked, her eyes widening.

I gave her an infuriatingly dopey smile.

'Nothing to worry about, Anthea,' said Florence, putting her hand over Mum's. 'We're all friends here.'

That's right, Florence. Play the senile card.

'How is your steak, Effy?' said Aldo. I'd forgotten it was there.

'Right, that's it,' said Mum suddenly, snatching my glass away. 'You're going to make yourself ill. Eat your food.'

I was about to grab my glass back off her when the pianist launched into something new. I didn't recognise it, but Florence clasped her hands together in, like, musical fucking rapture. I got up and started swaying and dancing, my eyes closed.

'Sit down, for Christ's sake,' hissed my mum.

Ignoring her, I took hold of Aldo's hands. 'Dance with me,' I said, trying to pull him up. He smelled lovely.

Aldo laughed. 'I think perhaps you're not used to Italian wine.'

He gently pulled his hands away from mine, and I felt

myself swaying, I was drunker than I thought. I sat down on the floor and laughed. I felt Mum's hands on my shoulders. She put her mouth close to my ear and said, 'You need to get up now. Everything's going to be fine, but you need to get up. You're embarrassing yourself.'

'I'm trying to have fun,' I said. 'Don't spoil it.'

His lips, his hands, my brown-eyed boy.

Then Aldo came and knelt beside me. 'Let me help you up, Effy,' he said. 'You seem to have fallen down.' He put his hands under my elbows and tried to lift me, but just succeeded in lifting my arms above my head. Made me laugh.

As I was clambering up a waiter appeared and said, in English, 'Can I get your daughter a glass of water?'

Daughter?! I laughed out loud and said, 'Yeah right. He's my daddy. He, like, spanks me . . . when I'm naughty, but if I'm a good girl he'll give me a fucking good seeing-to.'

'Effy!' said Mum. She put her hands over her eyes. Mortified. 'For Christ's sake, you're going to get us thrown out.'

I glanced at Florence, who was the only one I was remotely worried about offending, but she was looking at me with a kind of half smile on her face. What was her game?

Then Mum's prediction came true and we were thrown out. Some English hotel guests had complained, apparently. Like I gave a shit.

As soon as we were outside Mum turned to Aldo and said, 'I am so sorry about Effy. I don't know what got into her.'

I waved my hands in front of her, so angry I felt like grabbing her hair and repeatedly banging her head against the wall. 'Hello? I am here,' I shouted.

Mum turned her face away from me. 'Your breath smells,' she said.

'What do you care?' I muttered. 'Trying to impress him, are you? Piss off.'

'I'd love to,' she said, her face red. 'But for better or worse I'm your mother, and I can't leave you in this state.'

How touching. There was stalemate. Me sitting on the pavement wishing I'd picked up the still half-full wine bottle from the table.

A movement made me look up. Florence had stumbled. 'Oh dear,' she said. 'I feel a little unwell. Too much wine. Anthea dear, would you take me home?'

'Of course,' said Mum. 'We'll all go. But are you OK? Should we find a doctor?'

'Oh no, no need for that. I just need my pills and my bed. And there's no need for you all to cut short your day. I'm sure Aldo won't mind looking after Effy.'

She looked at Aldo, who quickly said, 'Of course . . . Effy and I will stay and drink plenty of black coffee and eat lots of cake.'

'So that's settled then,' said Florence, rather too perkily. And was that a *wink* she just gave me? Fucking sly old bird.

Mum took Florence's arm and turned to Aldo. 'I'm so sorry about today,' she said. 'I feel terrible.'

'Please don't,' Aldo replied. 'There's no need.'

I could feel Mum looking at me, but I refused to meet her gaze. When I looked up, she and Florence were walking away.

Aldo sat down beside me, his hands resting on his raised knees. 'That was quite a performance,' he said. I looked at his ankles and feet, bare in leather loafers.

65

'Effy?'

'What?'

'I said, that was quite a performance.'

I shrugged and lit a cigarette and felt immediately nauseous. But that would pass.

'Are you . . . Are you in some kind of trouble?' said Aldo, clueless.

'Trouble?' I laughed humourlessly. 'Maybe that's one word for it.'

'Want to tell me?'

You really don't want to know.

'Doesn't matter,' I said solemnly. 'I just wanted someone to make me forget.' I shivered in spite of the heat.

Aldo moved closer to me. He took off his jacket and put it around my shoulders.

'Alcohol lowers your body temperature,' he said. He took a cigarette from my packet.

'I thought you disapproved of smoking?'

'I do. The affliction of the ex-smoker,' he said, cupping his cigarette behind his hand as he lit it. He exhaled. His hand shook slightly as he gave me back my lighter. 'I must admit that I am . . . unsettled by you, Effy,' he said, not looking at me but straight ahead.

'What do you mean?' I sounded more innocent than I felt. As he turned to face me my eyes fell to the belt on his trousers. I thought about my mouth on his cock and climbing on top of him, feeling him fill up my cunt.

Stop Effy. Don't do anything fucking stupid.

Aldo shook his head, stubbed out his fag and stood up. He put out his hand to pull me to my feet and towards him, putting his arms around me. 'Poor Effy,' he said.

I rested my head on his chest, smelled his smell and listened to his heart beat. I arched my back so my tits pressed into him and, when he didn't let go, reached down and put my hand on his crotch. He didn't push me away immediately, though; he waited a beat. In which time I had all I needed. The feel of him hard against my touch.

'You are a little drunk, Effy,' he said then, quietly. 'This is not what you want.'

'You don't know what I want,' I said hoarsely. 'You have no fucking idea.'

'Maybe not.' Aldo took another cigarette and lit it. 'But whether you want it or not, I am now going to buy you some strong coffee and something very sweet to eat.' He buttoned his jacket over my shoulders. 'Come on. You'll feel much better, I promise.'

Week Two

Naomi

Monday 10 August

The Caves, Bristol

'I've heard about your infantile sexathon,' I told Cook, as he buzzed around me like a horny wasp. 'And quite apart from the fact that I am no longer interested in cock, of any description, I am never, ever, not in a million years, not if hell freezes over, not if we were the last two humans left alive and only shagging you would save me from being eaten alive by some hideous new strain of bacteria, ever EVER going to let *your* cock anywhere near me. That clear?'

'You love it,' said Cook, taking a half-smoked spliff out of his back pocket. 'If I stopped trying to shag you, Campbell, you'd be gutted.' He zipped up his jacket, which was ripped up the underside of one arm.

'Aw, babe. You need someone to look after you.' I tugged at the ripped tartan lining. 'Not shag you.'

'Fucking bullshit,' he said pleasantly. 'Care to join me for a smoke?'

I spotted a vacant-looking JJ across the floor.

'Nah. Think I'll go and chat to Jeremiah,' I told him. 'Get some decent adult conversation.'

'Fair dos, Lady Naomi.' Cook headed towards the exit. 'But if you see Frederick, tell him he's got some catching up to do. Cookie's steaming ahead with the contest. Piece of piss, as usual.'

'I'm not getting involved. It's mindless and sad,' I said. 'But I'll send him your way and you can tell him.' I watched Cook disappear through the door before I went to find JJ.

I'd come out tonight to reclaim myself. The bit of myself that was engaged in pining for my girl. But all that happened was I found myself looking for her in the crowds. Fucking ridiculous. I'm losing it.

I felt someone nudging me in the back. JJ appeared behind me.

'Want to see a trick?' he said eagerly, starting to put his hands in his pockets.

'No, JJ. I really don't.' I dragged one hand out. 'But let's go and sit down somewhere.'

'Really?' He looked confused.

'For a chat,' I said, laughing. 'No funny business.'

JJ followed me to a kind of seedy-looking banquette by the wall. A couple vigorously rubbing each other's bodyparts were sprawled out on it. I tapped the girl's shoulder, gave her my infamous death stare and they both shuffled to the side to let us sit down.

JJ looked simultaneously apologetic and impressed.

'So, what's going on with Cook and this twisted sex competition, then?' I said. 'I mean, can't he just have a good cry like a normal human being?'

'Yes,' said JJ. 'It is a little overblown, granted.'

As if to prove Jay's point, Cook reappeared, this time with a girl in tow. He led her over to the sofa immediately in front of JJ and me, and stuck his tongue down her throat. Nice one, Cook. Subtle.

JJ peered at them. 'He was with her when we were here last week. I recognise the snake tattoo on her foot. Shall we sit somewhere else?'

'I'm not moving now. Let's just pretend they're not here.' I still had a plastic glass half-full of warm vodka and tonic. I took a large slug. JJ sipped his water.

'Why don't you drink, JJ?' I asked him.

He looked at me, then quickly looked away again. 'Don't much like the taste,' he said.

'Is that the real reason?'

JJ smiled nervously. 'It's one of them.' He took a sip of his water. 'So, Naomi . . .'

I interrupted him, deciding to put him out of his misery. 'JJ, you know I'm cool with what happened between you and Emily.'

He looked down at the bottle in his hands and started peeling off the label. 'Are you? I mean . . . good, I'm glad. It was very much an act of charity. On her part, obviously.'

I watched him nervously picking at his bottle. 'She likes you,' I said. 'I didn't hear any complaints, either . . . you know, about the—'

JJ's whole face was suddenly bathed in pinky-red.

'Whatever,' he muttered. 'I understand when I'm being patronised, Naomi.'

'Fuck. No, JJ. I'm not patronising you. You're cleverer than the whole fucking lot of us,' I said, feeling clumsier by the second. 'Do you really think that shagging anything that moves makes you remotely special?' My eyes flickered briefly over to Cook. 'Or makes you happy?'

'It would make me ecstatically happy,' said JJ, finally putting down his bottle. 'To feel normal.'

I nodded. I knew what it was like to feel like everyone else is in on some big joke that you're not getting. I've felt like that pretty much all my life.

'You'll be fine,' I told him. 'I promise you.'

JJ accepted that with a half smile. 'In the meantime,' he sighed, gesturing opposite us. 'I am merely here to observe . . .'

Cook was indulging in some totally over-the-top heavy petting. His hand was inside the front zip of the girl's jeans as she writhed about noisily on his lap.

JJ and I exchanged amused glances. I felt a presence beside me.

'All right?' Freddie flopped down between us. 'Where's Cook?'

'Right in front of you,' replied JJ.

'Fuck, already?' Freddie sighed and let his head fall back until he was staring at the ceiling.

'Oh Freddie,' I said. 'Cook thinks you should get your arse in gear if you stand a chance of winning your little game,' I told him. 'Just passing it on.'

'Thanks.' Freddie looked everywhere but at the sight in front of us.

What a merry little bunch of monkeys we three made.

After a bit Freds suddenly sat up, banged his knees with his hands and said, 'So . . . how's it going with Emily?'

'OK. She's on holiday, with the rest of the fucking Addams family.'

He raised his eyebrows.

'They hate me. Particularly the evil twin.'

JJ leant across Freddie. 'It's strange. Even though they're identical I sometimes forget that Katie's Emily's sister,' he said. His face lit up: 'Hey Freds, we've had sexual intercourse with twins! It's like a porn film . . .' His smile dropped. 'I mean, from what I hear.'

Freddie wiped his hand over his face. 'Not funny,' he said. 'I still feel shit about that.'

'I wouldn't bother,' I said. 'Katie's a total bitch. She deserved everything she got.'

'She's not that bad,' replied Freddie. Then, seeing my expression, 'I mean, maybe she's got some issues and shit . . .'

'Right. Whereas Effy's a totally fucking well-adjusted human being,' I said, without thinking.

Freddie folded his arms across his chest and hunched his shoulders. 'What the fuck is that supposed to mean?'

'Nothing. You've got to question the mental health of someone who would knock a girl unconscious just so that she can fuck her boyfriend in a tent . . .' I sniffed. 'That's all.'

'You know fuck all about it,' said Freddie angrily. 'Just mind your own fucking business.'

JJ stared intently at the label on his water bottle.

'Fine,' I raised my plastic glass at him. 'Bye then.'

As I left half an hour later, I passed Freddie with a girl called Ashley, who lives next door but one to me and cuts my Mum's hair for her. They were leaning up against the side of the club. She had her skirt up round her waist, her legs wrapped tight around him, her tits on show. He was fucking her hard, his buttocks pumping fiercely back and forth as she panted into the air.

'Jesus,' I muttered to myself. 'Get me out of here.'

Emily

Tuesday 11 August

In bed, late

The door to the bedroom creaked open and her silhouette appeared. She moved barefoot over to her bed.

'Katie?' I whispered.

She looked across at me. 'You're still awake?'

'Couldn't sleep. Thinking about stuff.'

She didn't answer at first, just tugged off her dress and her bra and got under the sheet. I lay watching her.

'Why are you being weird?' she said.

'I was trying to have a conversation with you,' I said wearily. 'I won't bother again.'

Katie writhed a bit under her cover. 'It's bloody boiling in here.' She wriggled to get comfortable and bashed her pillow aggressively, eventually lying down to face me.

'So,' she said. 'Let's converse.'

'I was thinking about you today, that's all. You know, we haven't exactly been getting on lately.'

'Whose fault is that?' she said defensively. 'You've totally turned against me since you've been with her. And she hates my guts.'

'Yeah, right and you were always her biggest fucking fan, weren't you?'

'Well she was creepy. Staring at you all the time.'

'Katie.' I sat up. 'How many times do I have to tell you. It was *me*. Me who wanted Naomi. She didn't do anything.'

'Right.' Katie said, annoyingly breezy. 'Whatever you say.'

I needed to shut this down.

'So. You have a good night?' I asked, changing tack.

'You actually give a shit, do you?'

'For fuck's sake.'

'OK, then. If you really want to know. I spent the evening with a six-foot brick shithouse squaddy called Shane. No brain cells whatsoever, but abs of steel.' She paused. 'My jaw is in fucking agony. He held my head down while I was sucking him off. And he took bloody hours to come.'

Jesus. Katie.

'Well I hope he repaid the favour,' I said, lamely.

'Not really. Bit of a one-way street.' She yawned. 'But frankly, I was too exhausted to care.'

'Katie, why do you do this?'

'Because there's nothing else to do and I'm bored. Because it stops me thinking about how fucking ordinary I am.' She didn't look at me. 'Does that answer your question, you smug cow?'

'You don't need to—'

'Yes.' She pushed the sheet right off her now, and even in the moonlight I could see the massive bruise coming up on

78

her thigh. 'Yes, I do need to. I need to because I have nothing else, and I want to have something, you understand? Be good for something.'

I didn't know what to say. It was just too bloody bleak.

I got out of my bed and stood looking over hers.

'Shove over, then?' I said.

Katie moved to let me get in next to her. Carefully bypassing her bruise, I put one arm over her stomach and squeezed her waist.

'Don't try any of that lezzer stuff with me,' she said. 'I do draw the line somewhere.' But I felt her fingers threading through mine, and I smiled into the darkness.

'Tomorrow,' I said. 'We're gonna do something different.'

A pause. 'Like what?'

'Like, we're going to Paris. I'm bored with this shithole already.'

'Are you serious? You and me?'

'Why not? We used to quite like each other. Once.'

'True.' She sat up in bed and regarded me. 'OK. Let's do it.'

'Sorted.' I smiled, then sleepily turned over and closed my eyes.

'Night Em,' she said, turning the other way. 'Sleep tight.'

Katie

Wednesday 12 August

Bordeaux

'You ready yet?' asked Emily, appearing in the doorway.

'Yep.'

'I'll wait in the car,' she said. 'Don't forget the bloody kitchen sink.'

'Yeah, funny.'

She picked up her bag from the bed, and left me to it.

I stuffed another couple of bras and a dress into my bag and looked around the room to see if there was anything I'd missed. Then I saw her phone, lying next to where her bag had been. I stared at it for a second then quickly snatched it up, turned it to silent, and dropped it into my bag. It wouldn't kill her to be out of contact with Naomi for forty-eight hours.

'At fucking last . . . We're going to miss the train.' Emily shifted over as I hefted my bag in between us. Twice the size of hers. If she can survive on a pair of manky old

Converse and one of her disco granny outfits, then fine. But I had standards to maintain.

Dad started the car and Emily and I smiled awkwardly at each other.

'Ready?' he said.

'Ready.'

Bordeaux to Paris train, lunchtime

'Sirteen euro pleez . . . mademoiselle,' said the guy in the buffet car to my tits.

'*Merci beaucoup*,' I said, showing my dimples and widening my eyes. Might as well give the poor guy some wank material.

Back at our table Emily tucked into her *croque monsieur* as if she hadn't eaten in a month. I ate a couple of fries then sat back, sipping coffee and watching the flat French countryside whizzing past our window.

'So. Let's hope your fanny doesn't go into shock,' said Emily, smiling. 'What with the lack of action and everything.'

I leaned across the table and patted her hand reassuringly: 'Don't worry, I'll keep the noise down if I bring someone back to the hotel.'

Emily threw a screwed-up napkin at me. 'I'll fucking kill you. I booked a double room.' She stood up and reached her bag down from the overhead shelf. 'Do you want anything?'

I shook my head but she was suddenly burrowing manically in her bag.

'Your purse is there,' I said, pointing to the table.

'I know,' said Emily impatiently. 'I can't find my fucking phone.' She turned her bag upside down and shook it on to the table, raining down sweet wrappers, bits of fluff and a couple of tampons. One of them had lost half its wrapper. Yuck. She pulled the lining of her bag until it was hanging out.

Give it up, I thought. It's obviously not there.

'I can't believe this,' said Emily, practically crying. 'How could I have left my phone behind? It was on my bed, I know it was.'

I tried to look sympathetic. 'Don't worry, Em. It's only for a couple of days then you'll have it back.'

'I know . . .' She bit her lip and looked at the mess on the table. 'Can I borrow yours? Just for a minute, so I can tell her that I won't be calling for a couple of days.'

Fuck. I handed her my phone. I couldn't exactly say no.

'Thanks Kate. Won't be long,' she said, and walked up the aisle in the direction of the buffet, the phone already to her ear. I scowled but turned on my iPod and closed my eyes, letting Amy Winehouse and the movement of the train lull me to sleep. Or would have done, if my sister hadn't bashed into me on her way back.

'Ow, that fucking hurt,' I said, rubbing my arm.

'Sorry,' said Emily, her mouth full of Milka. 'Train jolted.'

'How d'you get on?' I said, pulling out my earphones.

'It went straight to voicemail,' said Emily. 'I'll try again later.'

I put my earphones back in. Suddenly I wasn't in the

mood for chatting. Anyway, a nap before Paris would set me up for the night ahead. Me and Emily hadn't gone clubbing together for months.

Naomi

Wednesday 12 August

Bristol

'Where the hell are you?' I listened to Emily's phone ring and ring and go to voicemail for the fifth fucking time. I didn't leave a message. I'd already left two.

I got up and paced my bedroom. I was so wound up, if someone had touched me I'd probably have burst into flames. My idea of a fucking nightmare. Me, getting so worked up over another human being.

Fuck you, Emily, I thought. I wish I'd never fucking met you.

'Naomi?' Mum's voice came from downstairs. 'Want some tea?'

I hesitated, took a few deep breaths. Calm down, calm down. It doesn't matter. She's probably at the beach or something. She's not deliberately not phoning you.

'Yeah. Be down in a sec.' I looked at myself in the mirror

and pushed my fingers through my hair. I'm growing it out. It's at the shit stage right now.

Apparently, so am I.

I got downstairs to find Kieran at the dining-room table. He was looking through a sheaf of papers. Mine could be in there somewhere.

'Give me an A, Kieran,' I said. 'Family discount.'

He looked troubled for a second, then laughed awkwardly.

'Ah, right. Yes . . . I see. Very funny, Naomi.' He picked up his mug and slurped some tea. 'You'd get one anyway, of course. You're my star pupil.'

'Yeah yeah,' I said. I tiptoed behind him to look over his shoulder. 'Let's have a look.'

He clutched the coursework to his chest. 'You've got to be fucking joking.'

I sat back down. 'Worth a try,' I sighed. For a few moments there I'd forgotten I was a paranoid wreck. Maybe hanging out with Kieran was the way to go. 'Where's Mum?' I asked him.

'What? Oh she's . . . she's . . .' he began absent-mindedly. He was circling a paragraph in red pen.

I waited. He finished scribbling in the margin and looked up. 'Ah, yes. Sorry. She's out in the garden I think . . . doing something or . . .' He trailed off again.

I gave up and poured myself some tea. We sat in what you'd call companionable silence for five minutes, until he finally put the lid back on his pen and stuffed the papers in his tatty old leather bag.

'So, Naomi,' he said brightly. 'What are you going to do with the rest of your life?'

I puffed my cheeks then blew all the air out. 'Funny you should say that.'

He regarded me seriously. 'You strike me as the kind of girl who'd have a "plan",' he said, making air quotes with his fingers.

My lips twitched. What a tosser. A well-meaning tosser. He was still gazing at me undeterred.

I exhaled loudly again. 'I did, kind of.'

'Did?'

'Do. Did. Whatever,' I said, rocking on my chair.

'Well, are you applying to universities next term?' he continued.

'Is this an official careers interview?' I said, beginning to feel irritated. Kieran smiled, but didn't answer. 'Yes I will probably be applying to uni,' I said, finally.

'Probably?'

'I don't fucking know, OK? I don't know what I'm going to do.' I put my head in my hands.

Bloody Emily. Making me unsure.

I lifted my head. Kieran was skinning up. 'Here,' he said, lighting the spliff and handing it to me. 'Try to chillax, or whatever you young people say.'

This time I laughed out loud. 'We certainly don't fucking say that!'

Kieran shrugged good-naturedly. He bounced his palms lightly off the table like he was weighing up whether or not to say something.

'Come on,' I said. 'Out with it.'

He gestured for the spliff. 'Look, it's none of my business but it seems to me that if you didn't apply for university you'd be betraying yourself.' He paused to have a toke. 'You have ambition, Naomi, that's fucking obvious. And it's not aimless "I want to be famous" shite. It's real. You have the potential and, while you don't necessarily need to go to university to achieve what you want, I think that that's where you want to start. If you deny yourself that . . .' He tailed off and got up from the table. He started rooting around in the Pile of Stuff by the toaster and took out a piece of paper from among the takeaway menus, bills and issues-based flyers that Mum had yet to Blu-Tack to the windows.

I could feel something stirring in me. I was flattered. By Kieran, of all people. Flattered; and embarrassed.

'Here,' he said. 'I printed this out for you.'

It was advertising an open day right here in Bristol for politics courses at Yale, as in big-name American university.

'Nothing to lose,' said Kieran.

'Maybe,' I said nonchalantly, staring at the ad, absorbing every detail.

'Up to you, of course.' He dragged on the last bit of spliff and stubbed it out in the ashtray. 'But clarity of thought is vital at this point in your life. However seductive certain . . . distractions might seem . . .'

My head was doing total fucking battle with my heart. This plan did not include Emily. But Emily had made me happier than I'd ever been.

'Thanks, Kieran,' I said, putting the ad in my bag. 'I'll give it some serious thought.'

I went back upstairs and lay on my bed. I dug the ad out of my bag again and scanned it. Excitement and possibility mingled with guilt. I picked up my phone and pressed redial.

'Hi, this is Emily. Not here. Back soon. You know what to do!'

I sighed heavily and turned on to my back.

'Don't do this to me, please,' I whispered, still clutching the future in my hand.

Katie

Wednesday 12 August

Hotel, evening

'Why can't you make an effort?' I asked my sister, taking in her wrinkled grey shirt-dress and Converse. 'We're in Paris, for fuck's sake. As in Parisian chic?' I gestured to myself, looking hot (although I say so myself) in LBD and scarlet heels. Didn't it bother her that I looked so much better than her?

Emily jumped up from the bed where she'd been reading while I got ready. 'This is me, Katie,' she said, opening the door. 'Deal with it.'

Why didn't she just put on some dungarees and show off her armpit hair? Go the whole fucking hog.

I really didn't get her.

But outside the hotel we both cheered up. Hard to be mardy on a summer night in Paris, and it was nice to be just the two of us again.

'What's this place again?' I asked. Emily was following a

map she'd torn out of the guidebook.

'Café Baroc. Eighties night,' she said, turning the page around to get her bearings.

'Is it far?'

'About a . . . fifteen-minute walk?'

'Fucking hell Emily, these shoes are crippling me. Can't we get a cab?'

'If you see one, feel free to flag it down,' she replied, handing me the bottle of red we'd picked up earlier. I had a swig and passed it back.

'Don't worry,' she said dryly. 'I'll hold it.'

The club was OK. A bit cheesy – and I'm not getting the whole French bloke vibe thing. A couple of them looked me up and down when we arrived, but not in the way boys back home do. It was like they were a bit fucking superior. It was the older blokes who seemed most interested. Dream on. I'm not touching a saggy arse, no matter how much Eau Savage he's emptied over him. I felt a bit depressed, to be honest. It was like no matter how much I drank, I wasn't getting pissed. Emily seemed totally happy just dancing by herself, not looking at anyone around us. But I didn't know what to do with myself. I'd gone from feeling irresistible to feeling like a fucking waste of space.

Emily grabbed hold of my hands. 'What's the matter?' she said. 'You were really up for this earlier.'

'Yeah.' I tried smiling but my mouth wasn't co-operating. 'I was. I am.' I danced awkwardly in front of her. It was like we were ten years old, at the end-of-term disco or something.

'Katie?' Emily moved closer. 'Why can't you just relax?'

She held out her bottle of fruit beer. 'Have a drink.'

I took a swig. Nothing. I felt this wave of loneliness, of the complete pointlessness of me. I couldn't help myself. Suddenly the tears were rolling down my face.

'Katie?' Emily stopped dancing. 'Babe, what's the matter?' She put her arms around me. I smelt her familiar musky smell and I clung on to her tighter.

'It's . . . nothing. I'm fine,' I wiped my face. 'I'm just being a twat.'

'Come on.' Emily led me to a bench by the bar. 'It'll be OK, Katie,' she said. 'It's just a weird time at the moment.' She finished her beer. 'It's fucking weird for me, too, you know . . .'

I wondered how long it would take her.

I shrugged, feeling a million miles away from her again. 'Yeah, well. Enjoy it while it lasts.'

Emily's eyes narrowed. 'What's that supposed to mean?'

'Nothing lasts, that's all,' I said, dry-eyed again. 'You can't rely on anyone.'

'Yes you can . . .' she said, looking unsure. 'Not everyone's a flaky bastard.' She chewed her lip. 'What's the time?'

'Midnight,' I said, checking my phone.

'Can I borrow that?'

I held it behind my back. 'Not now, Em. She'll be asleep. Wait till morning.'

'Oh come on. I'll just leave a message.'

I sighed heavily and handed over my phone, and watched as Emily left the fifth message that day. I felt a twinge of guilt.

Was it really so bad that Emily was happy?

91

Back at the hotel we sat up in bed drinking wine and eating those sponge fingers you get in French supermarkets.

'My teeth have gone funny,' said Emily, rubbing them with her fingertips.

'That'll be the cheap cake,' I said. 'And the two-euro wine, and the disgusting sweet beer.'

Emily clinked her glass on mine drunkenly. 'No one could accuse us of being classy.'

'Speak for yourself,' I said, hiccupping.

'Fair enough.' Her eyes glanced at my phone on the bed. I shoved it out of sight.

'I wonder why Naomi isn't getting back to you,' I said. 'Still. Maybe she's not the type to hang around moping and shit? She's harder than that.'

Emily fell back on the bed. 'Give it a rest, Katie.'

'Then again,' I carried on. 'Didn't you say she didn't like being labelled . . . as gay or whatever? She's probably a bit freaked out.'

There was complete silence. I held my breath.

'I'm going to bed,' said Emily coldly. She took another swig of wine.

'I'll never leave you, though.' I rubbed her leg. 'You'll always have me.'

'How sweet,' said Emily, handing me the wine and burrowing under the covers. 'Just leave me alone, would you?'

'Jesus fucking Christ,' I said to her back. 'You're the one who wanted us to come here. Now you're fucking shutting me out again.'

'You're a liar, Katie,' said Emily. 'Pretending you're interested in me and Naomi. You just want to put the knife in all the time. Can't help yourself. You're fucking jealous. It's not my fault your self-esteem is in the toilet and you have to make yourself feel better by letting anything that moves up your cunt.'

I lashed out and grabbed a handful of her hair, pressing my face close to hers.

'Well at least I'm not some twatty little dyke who can only get some other miserable fucking dyke to give her one. At least I'm getting proper cock.'

'No, you're a pathetic little tart,' Emily snarled. 'Just piss OFF!'

She pushed me away from her so forcefully I fell backwards off the bed. It fucking hurt. Another bruise to add to my collection. I said nothing. Just lay there for a while, shocked, until eventually I heard her snoring. I got up and moved in, like, slow motion to the bathroom.

Undressing in front of the full-length mirror, I averted my eyes from the bruises on my leg. When I'd taken off my make-up I looked at my bare face in the glass. A sad, ugly little cow stared back at me. I stuck my finger into my reflection.

'You're a stupid, lonely bitch. You'll never find someone to love you like that,' I told my face. 'No one would give a shit if you weren't here.'

I stared at my clothes on the floor.

There was nothing left for me.

Emily

Thursday 13 August

Paris hotel, morning

'Katie, hurry up,' I said to the bathroom door. 'I really, really need a wee.'

No answer. Jesus. Was she still sulking?

I banged on the door, which swung open to reveal an empty bathroom. I stared, confused.

What the fuck?

Maybe she's just gone out for a walk, or down to reception? I thought. I phoned reception, and after five minutes of laughably bad communication with the guy manning the desk, ascertained that Katie had not been seen since he had come on duty.

At 6am.

I put down the phone and sat taking deep breaths on the bed. Her side looked like it hadn't been slept in. I scanned the room. And she had taken all her things.

'Don't panic,' I whispered to myself. But where was she? I thought about the night before. Her in the club. Never seen her like that before. Kind of defeated. That horrible bitchy argument late at night. I was furious because she wouldn't let me use her phone. I brought my fist down hard on the bed. Fucking Katie, why did she have to be such a fucking drama queen? I went to my bag and pulled out some clothes. She couldn't have gone far.

I thought about phoning Mum, but decided to leave it a while. She'd only give me a bollocking for being horrid to poor little Katie. But I was shaking as I stood in the lift to go down. What if she'd been attacked? She was good at giving it the big feisty one, but she wasn't that tough.

I stabbed at the button for the ground floor. Hurry the fuck up!

I needed to get out and find my sister.

Looking for Katie

'*Ma soeur est perdu*,' I said for the hundredth time. '*Elle est comme moi.*' I pointed to my face. '*Vous avez elle vu?*'

Fuck knew if that was right, but people seemed to get the idea. The girl behind the till shrugged. Nope, she hadn't seen her either. No one had seen her. I didn't even know why I was asking in this shop, except it was near our hotel. Racks of dusty vintage clothes were so not Katie's thing.

I gave up. My stomach rumbled loudly. '*Excusez moi,*' I muttered to a customer just coming in to the shop.

I really needed to get something to eat. I felt like I was about to pass out.

I walked for a block until I came across a quiet little café on the corner of the street. I pushed through the door. It was tiny, the walls covered with giant canvases of contemporary art, plants everywhere, and a mismatched collection of tables and chairs. Bashed-up velvet cushions were strewn over an old leather sofa and there was an ancient jukebox in the corner. Sweet. I liked it.

A tall, severe-looking girl wearing a tight leather dress was making coffee behind the counter. She looked up and smiled at me as I eyed the array of giant pastries on the bar.

'*Bonjour . . . Ca va?*' said the waitress, smiling. '*Qu'est-ce que tu veux, cherie?*'

'*Ca va,*' I smiled back, climbing up on to a counter stool by the window. '*Un pain au raisin et . . . un café au lait,*' I pointed at the pastry for good measure. '*Merci.*'

A couple of girls were sitting along from me at the bar, deep in conversation. As I sat waiting for my food, one of them raised her head to look me up and down. I looked away, feeling self-conscious.

When my pastry arrived I couldn't get it into my mouth fast enough. I chewed quickly, staring ahead of me. Some jazz was playing quietly in the background. Soporific. I took gulps of my coffee, and then sat back. A wave of tiredness washed over me, but I fought it. I needed more caffeine. I couldn't afford to relax.

'OK!' hissed the girl beside me to her friend in English. She started taking money out of her purse and shoved some coins on the counter. 'There is nothing more to say.

I can't do this now . . .' She gathered up her bag and jumped off the stool.

'Sara, wait,' said her friend. 'Call me—' But the girl was outside already.

I quickly studied the coffee machine.

'*S'il vous plait*,' I asked the waitress. '*Un autre* . . .' I pointed at my coffee.

'*Oui*,' she said, friendly. 'You are English?'

I nodded. 'That obvious?'

The girl next to me swivelled round on her stool. 'You know, your French is really OK,' she said. 'At least you make the effort.'

She exchanged a strange look with the waitress, who had started making my coffee.

'So,' said the girl. 'My name is Anna.'

'Emily.' We stuck our hands out at each other awkwardly and shook.

'You are on holiday?' She was a few years older than me, with dark blonde hair in a kind of forties movie-star swathe and immaculate red lipstick.

'Just a few days in Paris . . .' I said. 'I am actually looking for my sister . . . She disappeared last night.'

Her eyes widened. 'Oh no,' she said, concerned. 'Do you have a picture? Maybe it is I have seen her someplace.'

I shook my head. 'I don't have a photo, but she's my twin. She looks like me.'

Anna leaned forward and examined my face. '*Non*,' she said gently after a minute. 'I have not seen another like you. I'm sorry.'

She spoke in French to the waitress, who had placed a

second cup of coffee in front of me and was wiping one of the tables.

Anna turned back to me. 'Bene says she saw a girl – with hair like yours, pale skin – at around 2am last night. It was dark, but she had a shiny bag with her. A very short dress?'

'That's her!' I said, excited. 'Where was she?'

'Around Rue Cavare,' said Bene, coming over and moving her cloth over the counter. 'She was a little upset. My friends and I were going to ask her if she was all right. But she ran away from us.'

Poor Katie. I closed my eyes. *I told her to piss off. And she did.*

Anna watched my face. 'Look, I can ask around today,' she said. 'Maybe someone else has seen your sister.' She patted my knee. 'Someone as pretty as you . . . They are bound to have noticed her.'

Of all the bars in all the world.

'Thanks, that's really kind.'

She waved her hand. '*De rien.* It's nothing. I am glad to help you.'

I watched her skilfully applying fresh lipstick. 'Was that your girlfriend, before?'

Anna put her lipstick away. 'My ex-girlfriend,' she said, shrugging. 'As of just now.' She sighed. 'Oh, these fucking relationships. They wear me out.'

I laughed. 'I know what you mean.'

'You have a girlfriend?' Anna said quickly, casually.

'I . . . er. Yes. Very new.' I was fucking blushing. 'She's back in England.'

'She's a lucky girl.' Anna watched me fumbling with my cup. 'Listen.' She pushed a couple of notes towards Bene.

'I have a few hours off work today. I can take you to some places . . . where your sister might be?'

I hesitated. 'Are you sure? That would be brilliant.'

'Of course. When you have finished your drink I will help you.' She smiled. 'No problem at all.'

Ten minutes later, Anna and I were heading to her neighbourhood.

'We will start with the cafés and bars here,' she said briskly.

And we walked for miles, Anna firing machine-gun French at everyone we met and moving on in seconds. Nobody had seen Katie. I felt fear creeping over me. This was more than a sulk.

I must have looked as worried as I felt, because Anna put an arm loosely around me.

'Don't give up,' she said. 'Paris is bigger than you think. Let's stop and make another plan.' We were outside a building with windows painted black and gold.

'This is 3W, my favourite café.' She paused. 'It means Woman with Woman. We will stop for a drink.'

I felt uneasy. 'Thanks, but I need to keep looking for my sister.'

Anna sighed. She reached out and touched my cheek. 'I understand. But I would still like to help you. You look so alone.' She got something out of her purse. 'Here.' She handed me a thick business card with her name and a mobile phone number in embossed purple ink. 'If you change your mind I will be here this evening. From nine.'

'Thanks.' I doubted I'd ever see her again. Apart from the fact that my sister was somewhere in Paris, doing God knows what, there was something about Anna that made me uncomfortable. 'I'll see what I'm doing.'

I left Anna and found my way back to the hotel. It was three in the afternoon and Katie was nowhere to be seen.

It's OK, I told myself. She'll come back.

She has to come back.

Back at the hotel

I blew twenty euros on room service and lay back on one of the beds waiting for my food. I shifted uncomfortably: something hard was poking into my back. I delved around behind me, and my hand closed round a familiar object. My phone.

What. The. Fuck?

I stared at it, trying to work out when it was that I had lost consciousness and dreamt the past twenty-four hours. My phone was here? And who'd set it on silent'?

Katie. I'd seen her pulling the same thing on her boyfriends. Paranoid fucking kleptomania. She'd nicked my phone, hoping it would stop me and Naomi staying in touch.

You shouldn't have bothered, I thought. Naomi obviously doesn't give a fuck anyway.

In spite of her nasty little game, the thought of Katie wandering around Paris alone and miserable pretty much overrode my feelings about Naomi going AWOL. I couldn't get her crying in the club out of my head. Katie never does that. She's the confident one. And I'd just brushed it off, started crapping on about Naomi again. The thought that my invincible sister was falling apart was like someone attacking the ground beneath my feet.

I scrolled down my contacts to find Naomi's number, but the red light flashed once and the screen went black. My battery was gone. I couldn't even check for messages.

I growled in frustration. I'd have to use the phone in the room to call Mum. It would cost a fucking fortune, but this was an emergency.

The phone rang for ages. I was about to hang up when Mum answered, out of breath.

'Mum. It's me. Emily.'

'Hello darling . . .' She sounded confused. 'What's going on?'

'Katie's disappeared.'

A pause.

'Have you phoned her?' said Mum.

'Her number's in my phone and my bloody battery's dead,' I said, stopping at the truth. 'She's—'

Mum cut me off. 'What have you done now?'

'Nothing. We had a row,' I said. 'Believe it or not, I don't go out of my way to fucking alienate Katie. *I* fucking suggested going to Paris in the first place!'

'Don't swear, babe,' said Mum, sounding calmer. 'I know you're not doing it deliberately. But you do wind her up and she's vulnerable at the moment. Her confidence has been badly knocked.'

Way to make me feel like shit, Mum, I thought, closing my eyes. Fuck. What if Katie did something really stupid?

I heard Mum telling Dad to call Katie on her mobile, then to me she said, 'OK look, you stay there. She'll probably come back to the hotel.'

'OK, I'll book another night. Has Dad got through to her?'

'No, her phone's switched off.' Mum's voice wavered. 'I'm sure it will be fine. We'll keep trying her.'

'Mum?' I said. 'I'm sorry.'

'I've got to go,' said Mum quickly. 'I'll let you know as soon as she gets in touch.'

I sat staring at Katie's bed. 'Katie,' I whispered. 'Just come back, you silly bitch.'

I was woken by the hotel phone ringing. I sat up, disorientated.

'Hello?'

'Emily, it's Mum. Katie phoned us at last.'

'What? Where is she?' I was wide awake now.

'She's still in Paris,' said Mum. 'She sounded very strange. Very quiet.'

'Yeah?' I pulled my knees up to my chest, relief hitting me. 'What did she say?'

'She's not coming back to the villa for a while. Said something about taking a detour to Venice. Apparently your friend Effy is out there with her mother.' Mum paused. 'I've got to say, seems very odd to me . . . Considering what that bloody girl did to Katie.'

'Yeah,' I frowned. 'Really strange.' I couldn't help feeling a bit pissed off that Katie would rather spend time with Effy – of all people – than try and sort things with me.

'She must have her reasons, I suppose. The main thing is she's OK.'

'Exactly,' Mum said. 'Now, love, what time's your train?'

I thought for a moment. 'I'll come back tomorrow,' I said. 'I've already booked another night here. Might as well make use of it.'

'Right. Well I won't be happy till the two of you are where I can see you,' said Mum. She sighed. 'But I guess you're not children any more.'

'I'll be back tomorrow morning,' I said. 'Soon as I can.'

I put down the phone and thought for a minute. The drama was over. Silly cow, I thought, and bloody typical.

I needed a nice hot bath and a few vodkas. I wondered about calling more room service, looking at the phone. Then my eye caught Anna's card on the bedside table. I picked it up, flicking it back and forth between my fingers.

Katie was still alive. Noami didn't want to know. I was sick of feeling down.

It wouldn't hurt just to go along for a drink.

I made one more phone call.

Paris by night

It was five to nine but Anna was already waiting, wearing velvet flares, paisley shirt and enormous floppy hat. She should have looked a total fucking mess, but didn't.

'I am so glad you came,' she said, kissing me on both cheeks. 'Good news about your sister!'

103

'Yes,' I said wryly. 'A bit of a tantrum, that's all.'

Anna smiled, tucking her arm into mine.

'Don't you feel hot?' I asked, as we started walking.

'Yes, very,' she replied. 'But I look good, *non*?'

'Yeah. I like your hat.'

'And I love your outfit. It is adorable,' she said, taking in my vintage fifties prom dress. A last-minute addition to Paris packing, thank God. 'So, we go to *Violette*, the *plus branché* lesbian club in Paris. You would probably get in without me,' she admitted, looking me up and down. 'But you would have to queue.'

OK. Feeling slightly out of my depth, but nothing ventured . . .

Violette was bathed in purple light and heaving. Everywhere I looked there were girls: dancing, holding hands, laughing, kissing. No one looked at me as if I was a fake or didn't deserve to be there. I felt myself relax almost immediately. No dodgy looks, or whispers behind hands. It was just so normal.

'You like it?' shouted Anna, breaking my reverie.

'Yes!' I shouted back. 'It's great!'

Anna looked delighted, as if I'd given her a present, and took hold of my hand. 'Come on, I will introduce you to my friends.'

She led me around the bar, and through a heavy embroidered curtain to a smaller, more intimate-looking room.

'Anna!' shouted a voice from a group of girls by the window. She waved and led us over to the velvet-lined window seat, where four immaculately made-up girls were sprawled drinking wine. Two of them were topless. I tried not to stare.

'Everyone, this is my English friend Emily. Emily, these are *mes filles*.' She introduced them by name, but I only took in Danielle, a small pretty girl with an afro and a nipple ring who patted the space next to her. I sat down and someone else handed me a glass of wine. A third, smaller girl with a bob and wearing a man's tuxedo, shook out a packet of white powder onto a side table and cut it into six lines. The others took their turn but I held back. I'd never done coke before. I watched them all, with the rolled up fucking cardboard.

'You don't like?' asked Anna, smiling and gesturing to the final line. '*C'est tres pure.*'

I hesitated for just a couple of seconds. 'Um, OK. Thanks,' I said, kneeling down and somehow managing to get something up my nose.

I tucked myself back into the window seat, gazing happily around me. The Caves, with its plastic cups of vodka and aggressively hetero vibe seemed a world away, I thought, watching a tiny girl kissing a really tall woman in the other corner.

Anna finished a conversation with one of her friends and came to kneel down in front of me.

'So, petite Emily,' she said. 'I have something to show you.' She put a long, black-painted nail to her lips and, widening her eyes camply, whispered, 'A secret.'

She led us through a passage off the room, and then a fire escape door and up some back stairs. The music got steadily quieter until it was a reverberation by the time we reached the top, where Anna opened another door and we walked inside.

Crimson carpets, burgundy velvet sofas, maroon muslin drapes hanging from the ceiling. Red everywhere. Naomi would say it was like walking into hell. Fuck. Naomi. I couldn't let her go. But I was struggling to summon her because I seemed to be hearing and seeing everything so acutely. I felt like Alice in Wonderland. I burst out laughing. *Eat me!*

I glanced at Anna, who smiled and touched my hair, but I couldn't have said it out loud. The room was writhing with naked, or nearly naked women of all ages. Most of them were just talking, stroking each other, or kissing. My senses were on overdrive. I felt like I'd just had eighteen hours sleep and I could dance for ever.

Suddenly Danielle appeared next to me, with the others.

'*Ca va?*' she said, touching my waist. 'You like it here?'

I just smiled stupidly in response.

She looked over my head at Anna and then I felt both of their arms circling my waist.

'Come over here,' said Danielle, pushing me gently back on to a huge daybed.

I closed my eyes. Thought of Naomi. Pushed her out again.

It's just one night.

Suddenly music came over the speakers. Kind of ambient French pop. Anna started swaying, slowly pulling her clothes off. She had large, firm tits and a tiny waist. I couldn't take my eyes off her. She turned and moved towards Danielle.

Danielle was moving her hips, running her tongue over her perfectly made-up lips. I smiled, my heart speeding, but shook my head. I couldn't do anything. I could watch, that's all. Anna was in front of me again, and without taking her eyes off me, licked her finger and held herself so that I could see what she was doing. I shifted in my seat, watching as her finger moved faster and faster. In less than a minute she was coming, her eyes darting about, uncontrolled. Then she was finished, and her eyes closed for a few seconds. When she opened them again, she spoke to me.

'You want to have a go, Emily?' she said.

I shook my head. No way was I going to cheat on Naomi. As if reading my mind she said, 'It's fine, you can watch us … if you like.' She reached out to take Danielle's hand and pulled her down to the floor, where she began gently taking off her clothes. I looked around, but no one gave a shit. They were too busy.

Anna was kissing Danielle's neck, her eyes on me, then she moved down and started slowly circling her nipples with her tongue. I felt like I should look away, but I didn't want to. As Anna moved down between her legs, Danielle put her head back, her breathing coming out as little gasps as Anna got more forceful, her hands pinning down Danielle's legs. And then Danielle came, a thin layer of sweat all over her. I realised my own breathing had increased, my heartbeat loud in my ears. I shut my eyes, and then the music, the sounds of the room came back. When I opened them again Anna was watching me. She smiled: 'Did you like that Emily?'

I nodded.

'Good.' She stroked Danielle's cheek and then the two of them got dressed. After Anna had applied more lipstick, she put her hand out to me. 'Come on,' she said. 'We have ordered food.'

I stood up shakily and looked around me. The others were just sitting around chatting, sharing bowls of skinny French chips. Acting like it was a bloody housewives' coffee morning. My breathing had slowed down a little but my heart was still thumping in my chest. I felt weird. Anna and Danielle whispered something to each other and looked over at me. What the fuck were they saying? Suddenly I felt that these people were not my friends. Anna wasn't smiling any more. Or was I just being oversensitive?

I stayed for another hour, until midnight, but spent the time gazing vacantly around me adrenalised, half-listening to the girls' conversation. Once or twice I felt Anna's hand stroking the small of my back, but I twitched away from it. I drank two treble vodkas and started shivering. I had to leave now. I was starting to feel sad.

Back at the hotel I pulled off my clothes and climbed into bed without bothering to brush my teeth or take off my make-up. But I couldn't sleep. I lay staring at the ceiling, watching the shadow reflections of the street outside. I thought of Naomi. My Naomi. Her blonde hair, her pink lips, the funny squeaking noises she made when she slept.

I held my arm up at a right angle to my head and let it find its own balance. I suddenly felt lonely. I wanted my girlfriend in bed with me. Watching Anna and Danielle made me long to do that to my baby. I could never tell Naomi – it's not her kind of thing. She'd rip the piss out of the people in that club. This was my secret. And I hadn't done anything wrong. I'd just watched.

Turning on my side, I curled up under the covers and closed my eyes. Anyway, I thought, Naomi hasn't returned any of my fucking calls.

Emily

Friday 14 August

Back at the chalet

I slept all the way back from Paris. I was up at 8am to check out of the hotel. Nauseous and depressed. I wouldn't be doing coke again anytime soon.

As I stood at the reception desk, the events of the night before filtered back into my head. The cold light of day made the night before seem grotesque – I shuddered. I don't go for those obvious predators like Anna for a reason. They're usually a bit fucked up. I longed for Naomi. Just thinking about her nose and mouth twitching when she tries not to laugh made me feel desperate.

But I would never see any of those people again. I'd been careful not to give Anna any contact details. And anyway, I reminded myself for the hundredth time. Naomi was AWOL.

Mum was waiting at the station, working the Desperate Housewife look in purple Juicy tracksuit and jewelled flipflops. She looked me up and down.

'You haven't been walking round Paris in that get-up?' she asked, taking in my plimsolls and creased cotton harem pants. 'You must have given them all a right fright, sweetheart!'

I wasn't in the mood for a style counselling session from my mother. I had bigger fish to fry. We drove in silence back to the chalet, and as soon as we arrived I raced inside to plug in my phone charger. I drank nearly a litre of water, waiting for the connection to kick in.

Ten missed calls. All from Naomi. A mixture of relief and dread swept through me as I listened to the messages. At first they were soft and loving, Naomi babbling about Cook and Freddie's pathetic shagathon. Missing me. But after the fourth message she was hostile. 'If you're not too busy skinny-dipping with your boyfriend, give me a call some time.' By message ten, she was in full ice-queen mode. 'Fuck you, Emily. If you've got cold feet, at least have the guts to talk to me about it.'

Shit. I didn't get it. I'd told her about my phone being MIA. She had Katie's number. What the fuck had happened?

Nervously, I called her back. She picked up after thirty seconds, which is like fucking ages if you think about it.

'Yep.'

'Naomi.' My throat felt constricted, my voice breathy and nasal at the same time. 'I'm so sorry, babe. I don't know what happened. I didn't have my phone. But I gave you Katie's number. You didn't call me back.'

'You never phoned me.' Her voice was like ice. 'Once.'

111

'I did.' I was panicking now. 'I swear to God. I called you loads.'

'What's my number?'

'What?'

'What's my number, Emily? And don't look at your phone.'

'07793 . . . 23468,' I said haltingly. I always had trouble with those middle digits.

'Wrong. Wrong. Wrong,' said Naomi.

There was silence.

'Shit. I've been calling a complete stranger, then.' I closed my eyes. So, it was all a horrible misunderstanding. 'But my God, Naomi. I've had the weirdest fucking two days. You're not gonna belie—'

'Whatever,' she cut me off, coldly. 'Doesn't matter that you can't even remember my phone number. That you were too busy twatting about with your new friend to *double-check* my fucking number.'

'Listen, babe. Katie and I went to Paris. She nicked my phone, and then fucked off in the middle of the night. Just ran off. I spent the whole of yesterday out of my mind, looking for her.' I bit my lip, I wasn't going to think about last night. It never happened. 'And she only got in touch this morning to tell us where she is.' I paused, batting away that little white lie. 'So, sorry if I didn't have the wherewithal to chase you up. I was kind of caught up in a major fucking drama of my own.' I stopped and drew breath.

'So where is she?' said Naomi after a few seconds. 'Where's the silly cow now?'

'In Venice, with Effy.'

'You're fucking kidding me?'

'Nope. Maybe she wants "closure" or some shit like that?'

'Hmmm.' Naomi sighed. 'Well. I suppose that explains your neglect.'

I smiled into the phone. 'I haven't stopped thinking about you. I've missed you like hell. It's been frustrating for me, too, you know.'

'Yeah, yeah,' she said. 'I forgive you, Emily Fitch. I can see how the whole ridiculous pantomime has played out. All orchestrated by the toxic twin, as usual.'

That wasn't really fair. But better to just go along with it for now.

'Anyway,' said Naomi. 'I've got to go. Kieran's got some stuff for me to look at.'

'Right. What stuff?'

'Nothing much,' she said vaguely. 'Look . . . Let's speak this evening, yeah?'

'OK,' I said, hurt. 'Speak later. Love you.'

'Yeah, bye,' said Naomi. 'Later.' She hung up.

Serves you right, Emily, I told myself. Serves you fucking right.

Naomi

Friday 14 August

Uncle Keith's

'Well, this is fun,' I said, watching Cook stare bleakly into his pint. 'And I was hoping you'd cheer me up.'

He glanced up. 'Trouble in Lesbos?' he asked. 'Sorry, mate.' He sniffed lavishly, rubbing his nose against the sleeve of his filthy jumper.

Cook's 'Uncle' Keith appeared behind the bar. He hacked up a lungful of phlegm, and stuck a half-pint glass under one of the optics. His eyes roamed around the pub, settling on me and Cook. He raised his glass to us.

'Can't start the day without a Jack Daniels,' he called blearily. 'Or indeed a vigorous wank to that bird off of breakfast TV.'

He winked at us. Repulsive old fucker. I smiled tightly, turning back to Cook.

'What's up with you, then? Finally realised the futility of existence? The meaningless void that is casual sex?'

'Dunno. Just fucking bored with it all, man.' Cook finished his pint.

'Are you lonely?' I asked him.

He screwed up his nose, poked me in the belly with his finger. 'Fuck off. I don't get lonely. Make fucking sure of it.'

'Ah.' I opened a bag of Salt & Vinegar. 'Maybe that's the problem?' I eyed him: he looked like shit. 'Just forget about her,' I said. 'She's not worth it.'

'Who?'

'Don't be a twat. You know who I mean.' I emptied some crisps into my mouth. 'And shagging everything that moves. Anger issues. It's probably something to do with your mother, and consequently all women.' I sniffed. 'In my opinion.'

'Spare me your fucking psycho feminist bullshit,' Cook said, perking up a bit. 'Anyway. What's your problem? Your girlfriend will be home soon. You're sorted.'

'Yeah, well. It's not as simple as that,' I said cryptically.

'Eh? Emily been a naughty girl has she?' He sat up, looking gleeful. 'Come on. Tell Cookie.'

'No. I don't think so. It's not her. It's me.'

'*You*'ve been a naughty girl?'

'No,' I said, frustrated. 'It's about this whole couple thing.' I shifted uncomfortably. 'It's messing with my future.'

'Future? What the fuck are you thinking about the future for?' said Cook. 'It's the here and now, Princess. That's what's important.'

'But don't you wonder about what's ahead of you?' I asked him. 'Don't you have a plan?'

'Bollocks,' he snorted. 'What's the point?'

'The point is . . . education, passing your exams. Getting a job.' I looked at him. 'It's important.'

'Not for me,' he said firmly. 'I'm not like you. You're clever. I'm going to end up like my dad.'

'Oh don't be such a pussy,' I said angrily. 'That's fucking lame.'

Cook drummed his fingers on the table. 'Maybe I don't know where to start,' he said. 'I haven't got a fucking clue.' He looked at me, red-eyed, pale. 'But you, you're going places, Campbell. You know it. I know it. Emily knows it.'

'I love her,' I said blankly. 'What am I going to do?'

Cook shrugged. 'Dunno, babe,' he said, pointing at his empty glass. 'But you can get us another fucking pint, for starters. I'm skint.'

I stood at the bar and rewound my phone conversation with Em. It had all been a misunderstanding with the phone calls. She wouldn't lie to me. I was pretty sure of that. And I couldn't wait till I could see her. Hold her and kiss her. So why I had been so cold to her?

Was it me that was going to fuck this up?

Effy

Friday 14 August

Santa Lucia train station, Venice

The red hair came first, then the tarty stretch Lycra dress, and finally the pale little legs wiggling along on shiny red wedges. Like a D-list WAG channelling Betty fucking Boop. I watched as a few random sleazebags gawped gratefully at her cleavage and smiled to myself. Some things will never change.

Katie stopped and pushed her sunglasses on top of her head. Looking around her, clueless, and really small. Then suddenly the crowds parted and she had a clear view of me, leaning up by one of those machines that stamps your ticket for you.

'Effy.' She waved, heaved her bag over her shoulder and walked towards me. I raised my hand in a half-greeting.

'Fucking hell, I thought you'd blow me out,' she said, looking me up and down. 'But you're actually here.'

'Seems so,' I said, digging my hands into my skirt pockets.

'Come on, let's get out of here. I need a cigarette.'

I snaked quickly through the station, which opens out on to the Grand Canal, trying to decide where I could take her first.

'Amazing train journey – really fast,' said Katie, hurrying to keep up with me in her ridiculous shoes. 'And this place. Fuck. It's just like it is on the telly.'

'I know. It's surreal.' I slowed down, took out a fag and lit up. 'You get used to it, though.'

We crossed over a large bridge and headed in the direction of our apartment block. I wanted, needed, a drink of some kind. I'd managed to score some weed from the creepy guy in the bar across the road from our building, too. Enough for another few days. I couldn't get through this unaided. But I've got to admit, it wasn't totally bad to see Katie. There was something about her that was different.

Less of the fucking peacock. More of the sparrow.

After ten minutes we arrived at a little restaurant with tables and chairs under an awning outside. I'd been in there, once with Aldo, and once with Florence and Mum. The guy who ran it came outside and nodded at me.

'*Signorina*,' he said politely. '*Ciao*.'

'*Ciao*.' I turned to Katie. 'We can have a drink here before we go back to the apartment, yeah?'

'Great,' Katie said, a bit too brightly.

As we sat down I caught sight of her face. She looked fucking terrible. Huge bags under her eyes. Where was the heavy make-up? The glossy lips? The colour? Hadn't she just been sunning herself in Bordeaux?

'You look like shit,' I said brutally. 'If you don't mind me saying.'

Katie fanned her face with the menu. 'You don't give a toss if I mind or not,' she said calmly.

I smiled. 'Fair enough.' I picked up the wine list. 'Bottle of house red?'

Katie shrugged. 'Fine by me.'

'So,' I said after the waiter had brought us our wine. 'What are you doing here, then? I thought you hated my guts.'

She angled her face up to the sun. 'To be honest, I have no idea. I just needed to get the hell out of France.'

'You worked your way through the male population of Bordeaux already?' I said facetiously.

'That's hilarious.' She poured some more wine into our glasses. 'Actually, it got boring.'

'The shagging?'

'Kind of. And I had a huge row with Emily.'

'Right.' I looked through my glass at her. 'What about?'

A shadow fell over her face. 'I was really vile to her. I couldn't stop myself from winding her up about Naomi.' She fiddled with her sunglasses. 'Emily's changed. She's not my mousy little sister any more. She's not taking my shit.'

'So. What? She told you to fuck off and she never wants to see you again?' I was interested in spite of myself.

'More or less.' Katie stared into her glass, swilling the wine around slowly. 'I can't blame her. She's better off without me. Everything I touch turns to shit.'

I poured the rest of the bottle into her glass. 'Yeah, well,' I said. 'Maybe you're not the only one.'

Katie looked across at me, waiting for me to elaborate.

But I wasn't about to 'open up' to anyone. Least of all her.

'Let's go and have a smoke,' I said, patting the pocket of my denim mini.

Katie started digging round in her purse for money to pay the bill.

'My treat,' I said, wedging fifteen euros under the empty wine bottle. 'Least I can do.'

It was 9pm by the time we wandered back to the apartment. Katie had perked up no end after a couple of spliffs in a deserted little square, even if she did cough her guts up every time she inhaled. We steered clear of mentioning the obvious bond between us. Freddie. Instead, in a bizarre kind of parallel universe-type scenario, me and my nemesis actually found ourselves having a laugh, especially when we tried to negotiate the myriad fucking streets on our way home. Finally I pushed through the now familiar door to the stairwell. This time hoping that Aldo was not in the vicinity.

Silence. Good.

'It smells in here,' said Katie, wrinkling her nose. 'Like all damp and shit.'

'Get used to it, Princess,' I said. 'And if you think I'm carrying your fucking bag up two flights of stairs, you can think again.'

'I wondered how long it would take for your mean streak to kick in,' she said, puffing and panting behind me as we climbed.

As we entered the apartment, I heard voices coming from the kitchen. One male, one female. I tensed immediately.

'Effy? That you?' Mum shouted, way too fucking gregariously for my liking. 'You pick up your friend OK?' She appeared in the hall, as Katie dumped her bag and disappeared into the bathroom.

'Who's here?' I said petulantly, knowing the answer.

'Hello, Effy,' Aldo called out from the kitchen. 'We seem to be having an impromptu party . . . Your mother and I are shamefully drunk already.'

I can't leave the silly bitch alone for ten minutes, I thought, struggling to keep my patented expression of bored indifference. I hadn't seen much of Aldo since Lido. I assumed I'd scared the shit out of him by making a pass. *Me*, making a pass. Who fucking knew?

Not that I was worried. He needs time to get used to the idea, that's all.

'Aldo just popped in to say hello,' Mum said. 'But I already had a bottle open . . .'

Christ, she was shit-faced. I felt like slapping her.

'And now we're on our third . . . Oh, hello?'

She clocked Katie who'd emerged from the bathroom, having obviously applied several layers of foundation and lipgloss in about thirty seconds flat. 'Katie, isn't it?'

'Yeah, hi.' Katie gave an inane smile. Mum looked unsteadily from one to the other of us. I could hear Aldo speaking to someone on his phone. Softly, affectionately.

'Alfredo's giving his daughter a call,' said Mum, proprietorially. 'Come on through.'

I was twitching. Since when had she got the fucking lowdown on Aldo's kids?

Mum practically danced back into the kitchen. Some stupid Bossa Nova shit was playing on the radio. I turned to Katie.

121

'She really gets on my fucking nerves, just humour her,' I whispered.

'She's all right,' said Katie. 'This might be a laugh.'

She followed Mum and I heard the scrape of a chair as Aldo got up to greet her.

I stayed back for a minute, leaning against the shelves in the hallway, listening to Katie simpering up to Aldo.

Brilliant. A slut, a man-eater and a fit older man.

What the fuck had I been thinking?

Katie

Saturday 15 August

Effy's place, Venice

'Give me a break,' I heard Anthea saying. 'So we had a few drinks last night. What's the matter? You worried I might start having some fun?'

'I didn't say that.' Effy's voice. 'It's just . . .'

'Just what?'

'Nothing. Just you fucking try and take over, that's all.'

I got out of bed and tiptoed into the hall.

'Your friend Katie didn't seem to mind,' said Anthea. 'Pass me the kettle, would you?' She was running the tap now. 'And Alfredo enjoyed himself. We all did.'

'It's Aldo,' Effy said sulkily. 'Why do you keep calling him Alfredo?'

' 'Cause that's his fucking name, Effy.'

I moved towards the bathroom. As I reached the door, Effy appeared out of the kitchen.

'Hi,' I said nervously. 'All right?'

123

'Fine.' She didn't look it. 'Sleep OK?'

'Great.' I tugged at my vest top, hugged myself self-consciously. 'All right if I have a shower?'

'Do what you want. Just don't use all the hot water.'

We eyed each other, like a couple of rival species.

'I won't be long,' I told her, pushing the bathroom door open. 'All yours in a minute.'

'Want some breakfast, Katie?' Anthea called to me. 'Coffee?'

'Great. Thanks Anthea . . .' I shut the door and leaned back against it.

I should never have come here.

I'd walked for miles that night I left Emily in the hotel. Crying. People were coming home from clubs and bars, but I just kept my head down and pushed past them. Not even the cat calls from some boys crowding out of a pool hall made me look up. Not interested. Can't put it on tonight. Sorry. And then I just dissolved, became invisible, floating above everyone.

I ended up at the Gare du Nord. 5am. My legs were stiff. I holed up in the weirdly clean station toilets and slept in a cubicle till eight, when the cleaner banged on the door. Probably thought I was a prostitute. Fuck knows I looked like one. I washed my face and put on some make-up and felt human again.

But I still didn't know what I was doing. Where exactly I planned to go. I sat in the station café for a bit, just going over and over the night before. And I thought of the last time I was genuinely happy. I came up with a memory of about

124

three years ago. Me and Emily on the Water Ride at Alton Towers. Screaming into each other's faces, holding hands. Just the two of us. We were fifteen. Dad had bought us both iPods for our birthday. We'd put all the same music on both. But I'd chosen it. I chose everything.

I drank the rest of my coffee and wandered out of the station. Montmartre was nearby. It said so on all the street signs. I wandered in and out of musty old churches, sat on ancient, crumbling walls and then on a bench eating a McDonalds. I thought of Emily's face if she could see me now. 'A McDonalds? You come all the way to Paris and eat a Big Mac?'

By early evening, exhaustion from the night before set in. I thought about the station toilets. Telling myself this was some kind of shitty hobo adventure, I decided to spend another night in my special cubicle. It hadn't stunk too much of piss and bleach. It was as good a place as any. First thing in the morning I had to catch a train from Paris-Bercy. If all went to plan.

I got out my phone and scrolled down till I got to her name. A minute later I'd sent the message. I spent an hour waiting for her reply, wondering if she'd tell me to fuck off. I willed her not to. I needed her to end things, see. Finish it off.

Please Effy, you owe me one.

And now I'm here. The sky hasn't fallen down. The world is still turning. I'm still alive.

I'm slightly disappointed.

JJ

Saturday 15 August

JJ's bedroom

'Good lot of jizz that, GayJay,' said Cook, holding up a condom and examining it through one eye. He waved it in my face, laughing as I tried to move out of the way. 'Another tick on the Cook side of the score sheet, cheers very much.'

I handed him a tissue and my wastepaper basket. 'There are elements to my task that I find profoundly unsettling,' I said. 'Monitoring your seminal fluid being one of them.'

Cook gave me a look. 'It's the only way, Jeremiah,' he said. 'Unless you want to take position underneath my bollocks?' He raised an eyebrow.

'Obviously not.' I sunk my head into my hands. 'But I'm not sure . . . I'm not sure that relegation to the role of Shag Arbiter is helping me in my own pointless desire to make contact, sexually speaking, with a member of the opposite sex.'

Cook was watching me warily.

'That is to say it is making me feel like a stooge. A clown. A laughable, dismissable human being. It is simply reinforcing my status as the only adolescent male in this city not to have successfully and confidently scored with a willing and non-pitying female of my own age.' I got up and paced the room. 'Not that I am not depressingly resigned to this role. It is just that when I have you bringing used condoms to my house on a daily basis it is increasingly difficult to not explode in *sheer, frustrated jealousy.*' I paused to draw breath. 'In short, this is making me feel like shit.'

'Jaykins.' Cook stopped me in my tracks. 'It's just a stupid fucking game. We can forget about it.'

He put his arms around me, and I stood, awkwardly encircled.

'Sit down mate.'

Cook gestured to my bed and sat down next to me. Once my respiratory rate had returned to near normal, he squeezed my knee and grinned.

'Jesus man, your wanking arm must have muscles like Popeye's.'

'It's not funny.'

'Chill out Jay, we all do it,' said Cook. 'Nothing to be ashamed of.'

'I know that,' I said, irritably. 'I would just rather not discuss it with you, that's all.'

'All right mate, calm down.'

He got up from the bed and walked around my room, picking things up and putting them down again. He could never sit still, yet apparently I am the hyperactive one.

'So,' he said, addressing a Parkzone F4U Corsair RTF with

127

Spektrum Radio Gear, 'we'd better get you some action.'

'I'm not going to that brothel again,' I said.

'No, we're gonna find you a girl who'll shag you for free,' said Cook, picking up another, much rarer model aeroplane. I refrained from telling him to be careful. Red rag to a bull.

'Oh splendid,' I said, willing him not to break it. 'I'm sure she'll be dazzlingly attractive then.'

'Jay you crazy motherfucker, you crease me up,' said Cook, although he wasn't actually laughing. 'Seriously, leave it to me and Freds. We'll sort you out.'

'Why do I feel a sense of impending doom?' I said, sighing.

'Relax. It'll be sweet.'

I looked up at him. 'All right. But I refuse to keep score in your sex game any more.'

'If that's what you want.'

'OK, then. I am prepared to be complicit in this plan.' I rocked slightly back and forth on my bed. 'Now, please leave me alone. And take your "jizzy" condom with you.'

Cook slapped me affectionately on the back. 'Fair enough, Jay. And I'll sort it, don't you worry.'

And so it was that I found myself nervously approaching Ritzy's night club at 10pm that night. Freddie and Cook were already waiting, smoking weed around the back of the club. To say they looked encouragingly at me as I walked towards them would be overstating it, but they did their best.

'Fuck's sake JJ, stop vibrating,' said Freddie. 'It'll be fine.' He handed me his spliff. 'Have some of this, it'll relax you.'

128

Or interfere with my medication and turn me loony. I shook my head.

'Her name's Holly,' said Cook, grabbing the proffered spliff. 'And as far as she's concerned this is a blind date with our best mate, so keep those fruitloop tendencies in check, yeah?'

'Right, yes, fine, I'll try my best.'

'Calm, JJ, yeah? Caaaalm.'

'Calm, yes, calm calm calm.'

My two best friends looked at me with what I saw was genuine consternation. I took some slow, deep breaths. 'Wheeew. Right. I'm fine now. Let's do this.'

'Sure?' said Freddie. I nodded. 'OK.' And I followed them into the club.

But it soon transpired that I wasn't fine. The noise and crowds, which don't usually bother me, freaked me out. I needed to leave as soon as humanly possible.

It was unfortunate that I began to articulate this to Freddie just as Holly appeared. Fred cut me off.

'JJ, this is Holly. Holly, JJ.'

I should try to describe what she looked like, but I can't remember. I think she probably said hello, but all I can recall is the expression on her face as I started banging the side of my head with my fists.

'Sorry sorry sorry I can't do this I thought I could but I can't I'm sure you're lovely but really you don't want to have sex with me I can't do this can't do this can't do this can't do this can't do this . . .'

Freddie covered my fists with his own and held them at the side of my face, 'JJ, SNAP OUT OF IT. C'mon mate.

129

Calm down . . . Calm.'

My breathing slowed, just in time for me to hear Holly shouting her thanks to Cook for setting her up with a 'fucking special needs kid'. I pulled away and ran. Freddie tried to grab me, but I screamed at him to fuck off and next thing I knew I was at home gouging into my bedroom wall with a Biro.

I woke up a few hours later on the floor, still dressed. I looked at my phone. 5am. I pulled on my pyjamas and crawled into bed, but couldn't sleep. Thirty-seven minutes later I got up again, put my clothes back on and left the house, holding my breath as I closed the front door. I'd left my mum a note, but I still didn't want to wake her. I needed to walk.

'Hey, JJ!' It was Thomas, waiting at a bus stop.

'What are you doing up?' I asked, veering off my trajectory to join him.

'I have an early shift at work. And you?'

'Couldn't sleep,' I said, rocking on my heels.

'I see.'

We stood in silence for a few moments.

'Anyway,' he said. 'Here's my bus, so . . .'

'I'll come with you,' I said quickly, and hopped on.

Thomas shrugged and smiled. 'OK, that would be nice.'

We sat at the front upstairs: my favourite seat. I wiped the condensation off the window with my sleeve.

'So. How are things?' asked Thomas.

'Oh. You know. Cook and Freddie are competing to see who can have the most casual sex.' I breathed on the window, wrote my name with my finger. 'And I'm not.'

Thomas shook his head. 'Sex,' he said mysteriously. He gazed out of the foggy window. 'What is this obsession with sex?'

'You'd know if you weren't getting any,' I said. 'And had no prospect of ever getting any.'

Thomas tuned back to me. 'OK. I tell you something that perhaps makes you feel better,' he said. 'I am not having any sex either.'

'Really?' I said. 'But Pandora—?'

Thomas cut me off. 'No, Pandora very much wants us to. I don't. Not yet, anyway.'

'Yes well, I wish I had that problem,' I said, moodily.

'I think perhaps you wouldn't if you did,' said Thomas in a quiet voice.

For a few minutes we sat in silence. The movement of the bus had almost sent me to sleep when suddenly Thomas spoke, making me jump.

'You know, Cook is an empty person,' he said, angrily. 'He does not care about anyone, I think. He only cares about sex.'

I winced. Of course: I'd forgotten about Pandora's history with Cook.

'He is a bit shallow in that respect,' I conceded. Thomas raised an eyebrow. 'But he's not a bad person. There are reasons for his unorthodox approach to life . . .'

'Really.' Thomas sounded sceptical.

'Well, to put it bluntly, his dad's a selfish bastard who doesn't give a shit about him,' I said. 'Cook used to worship him.'

'Used to?' asked Thomas.

'I think the scales have fallen from his eyes, in that sense,' I said.

'I see,' said Thomas. 'I have lost my father, but at least I know that he was a good man.' He looked down at his bus pass, flicked the cover a few times. 'I did not know this. Poor Cook.' He went back to his bus-pass flicking. It was kind of hypnotic.

'So . . . what are you going to do about Panda?' I asked.

'I don't know,' said Thomas. 'I am struggling with doing the right thing.'

'How nice to have that luxury,' I said, pulling my hood up. 'But you're probably right to put your foot down. I should try that sometimes.'

Thomas grinned and gripped my shoulder. 'You are a good man, JJ,' he said. 'Your time will come. Be patient. It will come.'

Katie

Saturday 15 August

Effy's apartment, later

'So,' said Anthea, opening another packet of fags. 'What are you two up to this evening?'

Effy looked sideways at me and then back at her mum. 'Haven't decided yet. I thought Aldo might take us out somewhere. If he's around.' She stared at Anthea. 'He said something last night . . .'

'Did he?' Anthea blew out a stream of smoke. Gross. She must be on forty a day. 'Don't bug him, Effy . . . He might feel obliged.'

'Why the fuck would he feel obliged?' Effy waved the smoke out of her face. 'He likes me.'

'Of course he likes you. Doesn't mean you should take advantage. That's all.'

Anthea got up and started rooting around in a cupboard. She took out some glasses and put them on the table. Effy yawned aggressively. I watched the two of them. Like what the fuck was the vibe between those two?

She'd been in an OK mood till we'd got back to the apartment last night and found her mum getting pissed with Alfredo. For the rest of the night till Anthea went to bed she had a face like a slapped arse. And the two of them were buzzing round Alfredo like bees to the honey. *Très* fucking weird.

Then as soon as Anthea had disappeared Effy skinned up and Aldo had joined us as we sat on the little balcony smoking. Effy made a big deal out of sitting next to Aldo, touching her hair and laughing a lot. Amusing herself as usual. I was knackered, so I just sat trying to get comfortable on the metal chair.

'I used to do this a lot,' said Aldo, taking a toke on the spliff. 'When I was a student.' He smiled vaguely. 'When life stretched before me as—' he waved his hand around, groping for the words '—as this vast meadow of . . . of freedom and irresponsibility.' He passed the spliff over to Effy. 'I loved it. But there comes a time when it does not fit so well with . . . with the pursuit of a satisfying existence.' He looked across the balcony rail into oblivion. 'And of love.'

Effy coughed, stretched out her legs and traced down her thigh with one finger. One hand still holding the joint. His eyes followed her finger as it moved.

'So who did you love?' she asked.

Aldo rubbed his forehead. 'I was very much in love with a girl at university. Rosalla. She was . . . difficult. Very serious and very resistant to my advances. She was so beautiful.' He looked directly at us for the first time. 'She knew this, yet it didn't make her happy. It made her distrustful, actually. She did not think that any man truly liked her . . . Her remarkable looks got in the way.' He shook his head. 'But, beauty is not enough. There has to be more. And she was clever and thoughtful and fragile.' He looked away again. 'I wanted to take care of her.'

Effy was staring at him. She dropped the end of the spliff on to the concrete floor and put her hands over her knees. 'What happened to her?'

'She killed herself,' he said bleakly. 'She hanged herself in her room.'

'Fuck,' I murmured. Effy had gone pale.

'That is when I changed,' said Aldo. 'I stopped thinking of my life ahead as indulgent . . . an indulgent playing field. It seemed important not to waste it. Instead I decided to find and hold precious those things that Rosalla felt she could never have.'

Effy was rocking slightly in her chair. She drew her legs up now and sat hugging them. 'So, you forgot about Rosalla?' she said.

He shook his head. 'I think about her every day. But you have to leave a certain kind of love behind.' He paused. 'It will destroy you if you don't.'

Effy and I looked at each other silently. This was starting to weird me out.

'Anyone want another drink?' said Effy, getting to her feet. 'I got some whisky.'

I shook my head. 'Ugh. No thanks.'

'I'll have a small one, thank you,' said Aldo. I might have been stoned or whatever, but I'm sure his fingers touched the hem of her skirt as she brushed past him. I was beginning to

135

feel like a fucking minor part in the Effy and Aldo Show.

While Effy was getting the whisky, Aldo smiled at me. 'You are good friends with Effy?'

I hesitated. 'We know a lot of the same people,' I said, dodging the question.

'I think she needs her friends right now.' Aldo crossed his legs. 'She is not quite what she seems.'

'Right. Yeah,' I said awkwardly. 'Maybe.'

Effy appeared with two tumblers and a small bottle of whisky.

'I think I'm going to bed now,' I said, getting up, not knowing where that was.

'Right.' Effy lit a cigarette and waved it about in front of me. 'You're in my bed.' She gave a half smile, seeing the look on my face. 'Don't worry. You'll be perfectly safe.' She poured out a large measure of whisky for Aldo, and one for herself then glanced sideways at me. 'Don't wait up.'

Week Three

Effy

Monday 17 August

A gift shop

'What about one of these cute little churches?' said Katie, picking up a St Mark's Basilica.

We were standing in a horrible rip-off gift shop near the main square, looking for Aldo's birthday present.

'He lives here, you twit,' I said. 'He doesn't want some tourist tat.' I looked at the price. 'And it's twenty fucking euros.'

'Fine.' She put it back. 'Just hurry up and get something then.'

'One more place to try,' I told her. 'Nearly done.'

As we left the shop I looked at Mum's precious *Time Out* guide. 'It's just down here, I think.'

We turned into a quiet-looking street.

'I dunno why you don't just get him a box of cigars,' said Katie, wrinkling her nose as we pushed open the door of a second-hand bookshop. 'That's what I'd get for my dad.'

'Yeah, well. He's not your dad,' I said impatiently, wondering where to start looking for what I wanted. 'He's not all macho and shit.'

She looked sideways at me. 'No, of course he isn't,' she said dryly. She looked at the shelves overflowing with old books. 'I don't get these kinds of places. Why would you go to some smelly old bookshop when you can order what you want off Amazon?'

'It's history,' I said witheringly. 'And it smells good.'

'That's a matter of opinion.' She picked up a paperback with a picture of a knight in shining armour on the cover. 'What do you want anyway?'

Before I could answer a woman appeared from the back of the shop. She was small and pretty with dark cropped hair and little glasses. She spotted us and frowned, looking with disapproval at Katie's bling leopardskin mini and gold gladiators ensemble. The vulgar *Inglese*. If I hadn't shared her distaste, I would have told her to fuck right off. However, I wasn't leaving without what I came for.

'Can I help you?' she said snootily, in English.

'Hopefully,' I said. 'Do you have *Death in Venice*?'

'Always,' she said, obviously surprised, smiling more nicely now. 'What kind do you want?'

I looked blank.

'First edition, paperback, hardback?' she prompted.

'How much is a first edition?' I said.

'Two hundred euro . . . or I have a paperback edition from the nineteen-thirties for thirty-five euro.' She went to one of the shelves and picked a book straight out. 'Here,' she said. 'It is a little worn, but is excellent for the price.'

I turned the book over and over in my hands. It was beautiful. I stuck my nose in and inhaled.

Katie shook her head, totally nonplussed. 'Come on, Effy,' she said, moving towards the door. 'Make your mind up.'

Thirty-five euros. But the thought of giving him the book later on was sending darts of pleasure through me. I was happy.

'Thanks, I'll take it,' I said to the woman. 'Can you wrap it up for me?'

'I can't believe we're doing this,' said Katie, eyeing up a fit boy running towards us with his shirt off. 'Going to a fortieth birthday party, with like kids and shit.' She pulled down her skirt sheepishly as a couple of priests walked past glowering at her.

I laughed. 'Never fucking thought I'd see the day,' I said. 'Sister bloody Fitch.'

'Shut up,' she said good-humouredly. 'Anyway, what's the deal with that book, Effy?' She looked ahead of her. 'Thirty-five euros?'

'So?' I said. 'He's just been kind to me that's all.'

'Hmm.' Katie looked unconvinced. 'It's a bit over the top if you ask me.'

'I didn't though, did I?' I bristled. I'd been quite pleased to see Katie when she'd first arrived, but the novelty was beginning to wear thin. She was stupid, but not quite stupid enough. And that was the problem.

'Fuck, it's two forty-five,' I said catching sight of a clock above a bar. 'We'd better get back. Aldo's meeting us soon.'

Katie and I had been vegging at the kitchen table this morning when Aldo had arrived and told us about his birthday. We'd gone to the bar down the road yesterday, drunk spirits all night, and eaten nothing. Needless to say we weren't up for much, and Mum was pretending to be Mrs fucking Hospitable, bustling around getting Katie coffee and pastries. She's been in a much better mood the last few days. I should be grateful, but the thing about my mother is that she can't win either way, poor cow. She just winds me up. End of.

'Got everything you need?' she said perkily to Katie.

'Yeah, thanks Anthea.' Katie picked at a chocolate cannoli. 'I'm good.'

'Right then,' said Mum. She'd started wearing make-up again. 'I think I'll go and see how Florence is doing.'

I sat forward. 'I'll come,' I said. 'Haven't seen Florence for ages.'

'She's not well at the moment.' Mum examined her face in her compact, brushing some power over her nose. 'I'm a bit worried about her.'

'Who's Florence?' said Katie with her mouth half-full. She sprayed pastry over the table.

'She's a nice little old lady who lives downstairs,' I said primly.

Katie stared at me as Mum went into the hall. 'I'm seriously fucking worried about you Effy,' she said. 'You'll be volunteering at Sheltered Housing next.'

'Florence isn't some senile old bag,' I said. 'She's fun.'

'Riiiight,' said Katie. She finished her pastry. 'Whatever you say.'

I ignored her. 'Say hello to Flo,' I called to Mum.

The door opened and I heard voices. Aldo was here.

'Not him again,' said Katie, brushing her lips. 'He can't keep away.' She eyed me provocatively. 'He's obviously got a thing for someone around here.'

I was careful to look totally unaffected by that remark. I craned my head to listen to what Aldo and Mum were talking about.

After she'd gone to bed, Aldo and I had stayed up till two the night Katie arrived. Getting stoned and talking. He'd tried to quiz me about my life in Bristol, but I was vague.

'You must have a boyfriend back home?' he asked.

'Not really.' I put my feet up on his legs and he'd looked down at my toes, his hand hovering awkwardly, then settling on the arm of his chair. 'Not any more.'

'You broke someone's heart?' he said. 'Or did he break yours?'

'No one does that,' I said too quickly, then calmed down. 'It wasn't serious, that's all.' My conscience was giving me a right good kicking, but I rode it out. 'And it's over.'

Aldo looked down at his whisky. A silence very much prevailed.

'You know, you remind me so much of her,' he said after a while.

'Who?'

'Rosalla.' He shifted in his chair. 'So full of doubt in herself, so frightened to trust.'

I caught my breath, feeling exposed. 'I don't—'

'And beautiful, of course,' Aldo continued, cutting me off. 'Painfully beautiful.'

I was trembling slightly, but this was not the moment to drop my guard. However tempting.

Aldo regarded me silently, and I shifted my legs closer to his lap. I wanted to curl up on that lap so bad.

'You have so much time ahead of you,' he said. 'So many people to fall in love with.'

Am I in love now? I thought, confused. Do I love him? I shut my eyes as Freddie's eyes seemed to merge with Aldo's in my head.

'What about you?' I said, gathering myself. 'Will you fall in love again?'

He caught his breath, rubbing his chin slowly. 'Perhaps,' he said. He didn't look at me. 'If she is the right one.'

He swirled his drink, then drained his glass. I stared out across the dark quadrant. The sky was that amazing petrol blue you get on late summer nights.

'Come on,' Aldo said eventually, looking at his watch. 'It is time for me to go I think.' He paused. 'But I have had a great time tonight. Unexpectedly great. Thank you.'

I let him out and stood for a bit leaning against the apartment door. Savouring the last few minutes of our conversation. He's yours, I told myself, if you want him.

'No,' Mum was saying to Aldo now. 'I'm just going to check up on her . . . You go and say hello to the girls.'

Aldo appeared in the kitchen doorway. '*Buongiorno!*' he said brightly, beaming at us.

'Hiya,' said Katie, flatly.

'I'll get you some coffee,' I said, getting to my feet. Katie gazed at me, wide-eyed. 'And we have pastries this morning.'

Aldo sat down, opposite Katie. He put his newspaper on the table. 'Thank you,' he said. 'Just coffee for me.' He watched me as I heated up some milk. 'Actually, I have an invitation for you . . . for you both.'

'Yeah?' I said, my hand trembling slightly as I held the milk pan. The door to the apartment opened again and Mum appeared, breathlessly in the kitchen.

'Florence is asleep,' she told us. 'I'll go back later on.'

Aldo nodded. 'We must keep an eye on her.' He smiled at Anthea. 'I was just about to tell Effy and Katie that it is my birthday today . . . My fortieth, in fact.'

'Ah, a spring chicken!' said Mum. 'Happy birthday.'

'I'm meeting my children later on,' he said. 'To celebrate.' He looked at us all. 'If you have no plans, I'd love it if you came too?'

'That's kind,' said Mum. 'Really kind. But your kids don't want a strange woman hanging about.'

Got that one right, Mother.

'You two go, though,' she said. 'I'm going to catch up on some beauty sleep.' She laughed girlishly. 'Much needed. But we must have a birthday celebration this evening. We'll ask some of the other tenants along too. An apartment building party!'

Aldo inclined his head politely. 'That would be lovely, Anthea.'

Or, totally fucking lame. On the other hand, I thought, Aldo drunk and happy might not be a bad thing.

Aldo looked at me as he said, 'If you girls have no plans, you'd be welcome to come along with me this afternoon.'

'We'd love that,' I said quickly. 'What time?'

'I'll meet you in the lobby at three,' he said, staring at my cold nipples. 'Make sure you're ready for then.'

Aldo's ex-wife's house

Later

'I won't be long,' said Aldo.

We were on the mainland where his kids lived. He got out of the car and walked up to a modern white-painted apartment building with huge windows. A totally average-looking woman in jeans and T-shirt and no make-up opened the door. The ex-wife. She was pushed out of the way by two gorgeous brown-eyed children – a boy and a girl – who threw themselves at Aldo.

He gathered them up in his arms, covering them with kisses. A spasm of jealousy stabbed me, and I stared sullenly as Katie and I sat waiting in the car.

'Sweet,' said Katie. Then she clocked my face. 'If you like that kind of thing.'

The older one, the girl, unleashed a torrent of sulky Italian at Aldo when she saw me in the front seat.

'I'm sorry Effy,' said Aldo, at least having the grace to look embarrassed, 'I always let Mara sit in the front seat. Would you mind . . . ?'

Yes I fucking would.

But I got into the back with Katie, and the younger one, Bruno, got in next to me. Cosy. Aldo introduced us in a mix of Italian and English. Mara looked at me in particular with silent venom.

After twenty minutes of watching the child simper and paw Aldo in the front seat, we parked at what looked suspiciously like a laser-gun virtual-war kind of place.

'Oh, brilliant,' whispered Katie. 'This is so not my idea of a good time.'

'Try and make an effort,' I said, sweetly. 'For the kiddies.'

Katie was predictably crap at it. I suppose it's hard to fully participate when you have to keep stopping to see if your thong is visible. But I stalked my prey with admirable determination.

As soon as the kids got bored it was just me and Aldo on the dancefloor, as it were. I was working up a bit of a sweat dodging his aim, as he followed me through dark passageways. I flattened myself against a wall and waited for him to come past me, poking my finger into his back.

'Got you,' I said, keeping my finger there, at the bottom of his spine.

He turned, laughing. I brushed my hair off my face, and pushed my hips forward. 'Aren't you going to try and shoot me?' I asked slowly.

He stopped laughing, panting slightly. I licked my lips and pointed at his gun. 'Go on.'

Aldo smiled, one hand reached out and touched my waist, rubbing it, tickling me. I started wriggling, giggling like a kid. 'Don't . . .' I said. 'I'm really ticklish.'

'Are you indeed.' Aldo's hands firmly persisted, and I twisted in his grip, turning to push my arse into his groin. I felt his erection, and rubbed my buttocks against it.

He stopped moving. 'Effy—' he said, firmly pushing me forward. 'No.'

My heart was pounding, my whole body registering disappointment even before I did.

There was just the sound of our breathing. I didn't want to look behind me. I knew if I did I would try and kiss him.

I imagined how forcefully he would do that. I closed my eyes. Fuck. Fuck. Fuck.

'Pappy!' Mara's voice pierced the silence. 'Pappy!'

Aldo moved out in front of me, walking back down the passage. He turned.

'It's OK, don't worry.' He smiled. 'Now, come on. I had better get my children home.'

Birthday drinks

Later that evening

'A-ha, the birthday boy!' sang Mum, skipping over to Aldo and handing him a glass of Prosecco.

She'd pulled out all the stops, put tea lights on the windowsills and brought down the table from our kitchen, laid it with glasses, bottles of wine, bowls of nibbles and even a fucking cake. A chocolate thing with '40' in shards of white chocolate on top, which I thought was naff, but the birthday boy seemed pleased.

I watched him make small talk, shake hands, kiss cheeks. Thought: Flirt with him all you want. He's mine. There was something in the air – the anticipation of a future in which he would lick me from top to bottom. Fuck me everywhere.

He wasn't looking at me. I expected that. I liked it in fact. Our little secret.

I'd found a moment to give him his present, while Mum and Katie were busy elsewhere. I handed over his book in its wrapping, I couldn't wait to see his face when he opened it.

He raised his eyebrows. 'Effy. What is this?'

I said nothing. Gestured for him to open it.

He laughed, his face actually lit up. 'But this is a wonderful present! Thank you, darling Effy!' He put his arms around me. Kissed me again. Darling Effy. He held my arms and then my gaze, but quickly looked away. 'I will put this somewhere safe,' he said, turning to find a hiding place.

'Effy!' Mum's voice, panicky, came from the hallway. 'Alfredo!'

She rushed at us, took Aldo's arm. 'It's Florence,' she said breathlessly. 'You'd better come now, Alfredo. She's not waking up.'

Cook

Monday 17 August

Freddie's shed

'So, Freddie. How does it feel to be in the presence of a legend?' I asked him, taking a swig from a can of Stella.

He shook his head, a kind of half smile on his smug, pretty-boy face. 'You really are a sad bastard.'

'It's nothing personal.' I squeezed his knee. 'It's just the law of the fucking jungle, mate.' I put my feet up on the fire extinguisher. 'We all knew from the start how this would play out. I'll always get the snatch. They can't say no to the Cookie Monster.'

Freddie was bent over hugging himself like a girl. 'You should listen to yourself, mate. It's pathetic. Really.'

'You would say that because you're fucking losing.' I paused. 'Again.'

Freddie looked up sharply. 'It's all you've got, this, isn't it?' He stood up. 'But, seriously—' He suddenly lunged right into my face. '—does it make it all better, Cook? Does it actually—'

JJ stood up, wringing his hands together nervously. 'OK, Cook. Freddie. Let's not have this discussion now.' He attempted a jolly little smile. 'I mean, if we're going to get competitive, may I venture, again, that I am actually the only one to have had sex with a lesbian.'

We stared at him. 'Shut up, JJ.'

Silence.

'Anyway,' said Freddie. 'It's boring.'

'Ah. Now see, I've got a cracking idea to liven it up, my friend.' I rubbed my hands together.

'Do tell,' said Fred, dry as the fucking Gobi desert.

'Something to decide the winner, like. Once and for all. To reveal the true master of the craft.'

JJ and Freddie sighed simultaneously.

'What have you got in mind?' said Fred. 'A fucking questionnaire?'

I shook my head. 'A threesome.'

'What?' Fred had that fucking stuck-up look on his face.

'A threesome. You, me and a girl. We take it in turns to fuck her, then she gives feedback.'

Jay looked way out of his depth now. Freddie looked a bit pale.

'That's a fucking bridge too far mate,' he said. 'It's almost sick.'

'No, it's democracy.'

'Actually,' said JJ, 'the dictionary definition of democracy is—'

'Shut up, JJ,' said me and Freds, again.

'Well,' I said. 'You going to step up to the fucking plate,

151

Freddie. Or are you going to back down like a pussy?'

Freddie gave me a look of pure hatred. 'Fine,' he said coldly. 'Whatever. Let me know when you've found a girl who's up for it.'

'Already done it,' I said. 'Polly, the posh bird with the clit ring from the other night? Says she's been thinking about a *ménage a trois*. This is her lucky day, mate. Seven o'clock at her place, tonight.'

There was a moment's silence. JJ gave Freddie a sympathetic pat on the shoulder.

'That's great,' said Freddie. 'I can't tell you how much I'm looking forward to it.' He lit a fag and opened the door. 'Now get the fuck out of my shed.'

Freddie

Outside Polly's house

'Nice house,' said JJ, as the three of us stood outside the front door of Polly's place. 'Big.'

I rolled my eyes at him. Cook was in front, chest pushed out, one hand holding a bottle of Jack Daniels. I started to feel sick.

Cook turned and winked at me as we waited for the door to open. 'Bet she's got a mirror above her bed, right Freds? We can watch it all as it happens.'

Thanks for that visual, you cunt.

After a good thirty seconds Polly let us in. She was pretty,

152

in a posh kind of way. Long blonde hair, tanned skin, massive bit of bling round her neck.

'Cookie, babe!' she said, kissing a space about an inch from his face.

'All right darling?' Cook replied. 'Freddie. JJ,' he said, pointing to each of us in turn.

'Hi guys!' said Polly. 'Come in, I've made cocktails.'

As she walked away Cook leaned in to us and whispered, 'Not the sharpest tool in the box, but she goes like a fucking train.'

Polly showed us into what she called the den, where everything was white. Massive white sofas, white flowers, even a white telly.

'This must be a bugger to keep clean,' said JJ.

'Staff, GayJay,' said Cook. 'These people won't have cleaned anything in their whole fucking life.'

'Right, and you have?' I said.

'That's different. Squalor is my loyal friend,' he replied.

We sat in silence for a couple of minutes, Cook trying to get the TV to work, JJ looking at his hands and me wishing I was anywhere but here, about to do this.

'Here we are!' said Polly, carrying a tray with four cocktail glasses and a chrome shaker. 'Who's for Sex on the Beach?'

JJ looked worried. 'Not for me, thanks.'

'You do know it's a drink, Jay?' said Cook.

Polly laughed. 'Cookie, you're so funny!'

Yes. He's a fucking scream.

We sat holding our stupid pink drinks making small talk for like fifteen minutes, until Cook drained his glass and said,

153

'Right Poll. No offence but let's cut the crap. We all know why we're here. So if you could lead the way . . . ?'

Polly put her own glass down, suddenly serious. 'Yah, absolutely.'

We followed her out of the room, Cook chucking JJ the telly remote on the way. 'Here, find the porn channels. Have some fun of your own.'

Polly's bedroom was a nightmare in pink, with posters of boy bands on the walls and soft toys all over the bed. As if reading my mind she said, 'Sorry about all this. It's going to be decorated when my parents get back from India. They're bringing back some fucking *amazing* wallpaper made from native grasses. You have to water it and everything.'

'Fascinating,' said Cook. 'So anyway, let's get naked, yeah?'

He pushed her back on to the bed and started kissing her and pulling her clothes off. As I stood and watched her bra flying across the room, I realised I had no idea how threesomes worked. Like, would Cook have a go, then me? Or was it a dual effort? One of us at one end, the other at the other, sort of thing. I hoped Polly would take the lead a bit, 'cause Cook wasn't going to give me a look-in. All he cared about, apart from getting laid, was Polly voting him the best so he'd win his fucking game.

By now they were both naked and Polly was sucking him off. This wasn't right. This was just so fucking wrong. I was kind of mesmerised though; in fact I couldn't move.

Polly took her mouth away from his cock.

'Well don't fucking stop,' said Cook.

'Freddie's turn,' said Polly, pulling me over to the bed and undoing my jeans. 'Let's see what we have here, then,' she said.

Not a lot as it transpired.

I tried to maintain some dignity by saying nothing and kissing Polly instead. I reached down inside her knickers to stroke her, but my cock was not playing. Not even stirring. Probably because I didn't fancy her, and because Cook was craning his head to watch the work in progress.

'Fuck off,' I hissed at him over Polly's head.

He grinned, delighted.

Polly tapped me on the shoulder. 'Can I make a suggestion?'

I looked up. Cook raised an eyebrow.

She curled her knees under her, pursed her lips and looked at each of us for a moment.

'Kiss. Each other.'

That wiped the smile off Cook's face. It'd have done the same to me, except I wasn't smiling in the first place.

'No babe, no way. I'm not kissing him,' said Cook.

'Fair enough. Freddie wins, then.'

I turned to Cook. 'You told her about the game?'

He shrugged. 'Thought it would spice things up.' And then, turning to Polly, 'I said, didn't I? We fuck you, you tell us who's best. End of story.'

'No,' said Polly. 'All you said was that I have to tell you who, in my opinion, gets me off.' She smiled a sugar smile. 'And I'll decide that, by watching you two do it to each other. Got it?'

Cook laughed. 'Very funny, Poll. Lovin' your work. Now

just lie down like a good girl and let me lick you till you scream. Believe me, it won't take long.'

Polly shook her head. 'You're unbelievable. These are my terms: you and Freddie. The whole hog...' She leaned forward. 'Which means,' she said to Cook. 'Your cock up his arse.' She smiled at me. 'Or vice versa.' She sat watching the two of us. 'Up to you.'

'Sorry, it's just not going to happen,' I said. 'This is fucking bullshit.' I turned to Cook. 'You win.'

'Nah. Nah. This is not the plan,' said Cook, looking distressed. 'Come on, Polls. Play the game.'

She laughed nastily. 'Play *your* game you mean? Piss off.'

She didn't sound quite so posh now.

'You've got a fucking nerve,' Polly went on, pulling a T-shirt over her tits. She stabbed Cook in the chest with her finger. 'You shag me, steal my knickers so I have to go commando in PVC trousers, which by the way led to a fucking bout of thrush, then you call me and tell me you want a threesome just so you can win some juvenile little bet with your mate?' She picked up her jeans and put them on. 'And by the way, you're not that good.' She rocked her hand from side to side. 'You're so-so.' She stared at him. 'Didn't think I'd notice did you? Seeing as I'm not the "sharpest tool in the box".'

Cook started putting his clothes on. I stood awkwardly by her bedroom door.

Polly picked up his jacket and threw it at him. 'Close the door on your way out,' she said coolly. 'Twat.'

JJ was watching *Wife Swap* and flicking through *The Economist* but looked up when he heard us come in. 'That was quick,' he said.

'Shut up, Jay, we're going,' said Cook.

'But—'

'Just Shut. The fuck. Up,' screamed Cook.

JJ turned off the TV and followed us out of the front door.

'It's all right, JJ,' I whispered, tousling his hair. 'The game is over now.'

JJ

Two minutes later

'Right,' said Cook, recovering his spirits as we made our way down the road. 'Onwards and upwards, boys.'

I was about to make a tentative enquiry as to what had gone wrong, when someone thudded to the ground behind me. I spun round to see Cook's head snapping back, blood pouring from his nose. Freddie stood over him, panting.

'This,' he said, 'is over. We. Are. Over.' He crouched down and pulled Cook up by his T-shirt. 'You've fucking humiliated us all. Again. But for the last time, you get me? The last fucking time.'

'Listen Fred.' Cook was struggling to get his breath. He wiped the blood off his face with his sleeve. 'It's a minor fucking setback for the musketeers, that's all.'

'Fuck the musketeers,' sneered Freddie. 'I don't want to

157

know.' He stood up and kicked viciously at a stone. 'You're ill. You need help, mate.' He turned to walk away in the other direction.

I stood helplessly in the face of the impending apocalypse.

As I predicted, Cook was not happy with leaving it there. He got to his feet and charged at Freddie, shoving him hard with both hands. 'It wasn't my fucking fault, you silly twat. She was a psycho.'

Freddie turned round and shoved Cook back. 'No, she was a normal human being driven to unnatural acts by your extreme fucking cuntishness.' He pushed him twice to emphasise the latter two words. 'You're a menace to society.' He paused. 'You're never going to have her, you know. She's never going to choose you.'

Somehow I didn't think he was referring to Polly. I felt the blood rushing into my head. Any second now—

And then they were on the floor, grabbing each other, punching, arms flailing. No longer discernible as human beings. They were Fight. An angry jagged mass of dust and hair and violence.

I could feel it building inside me, like when Bruce Banner becomes the Incredible Hulk only it wasn't green skin and limitless strength I was heading towards. I jittered around the fight, whimpering, 'No no no no no no no no,' and then the tears came and my voice got louder and louder until I was shouting, screaming so hard that afterwards my throat was raw. 'FUCKING STOP IT FUCKING STOP IT NOW FUCKING STOP IT STOP IT STOP IT STOP IT FUCK FUCK STOP IT NOW PLEASE FUCKING STOP IT STOP IT STOP IT.'

Then I realised that someone was holding me. I opened my eyes and saw bobbly grey cotton. Cook's T-shirt. His hand was on the back of my head, holding me to his chest. He was talking to me. 'JJ, it's OK. Come on, mate, we've stopped. Everything's fine, I promise. You're OK.' I felt him kiss the top of my head. They'd stopped fighting. All the tension left my body and I sank to the pavement.

'C'mon Jay, it's OK. Please stop crying,' said Freddie, holding on to the top of my arm.

I took my hankie out of my sleeve and wiped my face.

Cook held me in a grip of iron. 'I love you, Jaykins. You're my family, yeah?' He turned to Freddie. 'You too, man. She's not going to change that.'

Freddie appeared unmoved. He started picking at his trainers. 'But she has.' He looked at the two of us, clinging to each other like a pair of bruised lovers. 'She did that months ago.'

'Ah, fuck her. She's gone.' Cook finally let go of me, to the relief of my aching limbs. He looked plaintively at Freddie. 'But you, me and JJ. We're still tight, man. We've got each other. Yeah?'

Freddie shrugged. 'Dunno any more. It's not that simple, mate.' He ran a hand through his hair. 'It's just not that fucking simple.'

Effy

Tuesday 18 August

Late afternoon in Venice

'Jesus, you want him so bad,' said Katie. She was looking at me with a kind of wonder. Like she was seeing someone different. Another me.

I lit a fag. 'Don't be ridiculous.'

'I'm not fucking blind.' She grabbed my cigarette and took a drag. Coughed melodramatically and handed it back. 'I've seen it before, remember?'

I gave her a blank look.

'Only that time, you made it just a bit more obvious by fucking him.' She hugged her knees. 'Freddie? While I was unconscious?'

I rubbed at my teeth, itchy from smoking and alcohol. 'I said I was sorry.'

'Only because you didn't want him to think you were a bitch. Which he did, by the way.'

'Did he? Suppose I was.'

'The look on your face when you saw how Aldo's kids are with him . . . The same fucking evils you used to give me.'

I sniffed. 'Bet you loved that,' I said. 'That you had Freddie and I didn't.'

She nodded. 'Yeah. I did actually, while it lasted. You were so fucking superior. You could have your pick. They all wanted you.' She smiled. 'Until one of them didn't.'

Fucking hell, my eyes were watering. Pull yourself together you idiot, I thought.

'Effy always has to get what she wants.' Katie kicked at the step with her heel.

'Look, are you going to build a bridge and fucking get over that, or what?' I said, picking up the bottle of wine at my feet. I took a huge slug. Felt the rush of alcohol.

'I already have.' She fiddled with the strap on her sandal. 'I know when I'm beat.' She watched me as I took another mouthful of wine. 'You want to give it a try. It's quite a relief actually.'

I didn't answer. I didn't have a cool comeback. I had nothing. I don't really know what it's like to be made a fool of. But when Freddie started shagging Katie . . . I was humiliated to say the least. Proper fucking show that was.

Katie Fitch. Desperate, needy Katie. I always thought that if those two adjectives were ever applied to me I really would kill myself. But that's how I felt sitting on those steps with her. Needy and desperate. It's like that shit didn't stay behind after all. It got on a plane, morphed, and followed me, and it's fucking swallowed me up.

Hardly surprising that Katie had sussed it. I'd been waiting for Aldo to come over again, after his party at our place last night. Waiting, agitated. A cat on a hot tin roof. Going over and over what had happened that day. Cringing when I thought about giving him that fucking book. Pathetic. So eager to please. I felt like a twitchy, paranoid mess. Kept making excuses to go downstairs, although he was never there.

And then when he had finally come half an hour ago, he'd been with *her*. All supportive and shit. Treated me like a fucking child. Well, I was acting like one.

I hated myself.

'Anyway, Florence might be back from hospital now,' said Katie, totally changing the subject. 'Now she's better.'

Florence had been taken away in an ambulance after the party. A mild stroke, they said. Mum had been with her all night.

'Yeah, I'll go and see her,' I said. I took out another cigarette, my hand trembling as I lit it.

'Effy?' Katie craned round to look at me. 'You OK?'

'Fine,' I said, just as my phone beeped. Mum probably. I took it out of my bag and clicked on my messages. Something flooded through me as I saw his name. Warmth? Cold? I don't know.

I swallowed and opened up the message. The first one for weeks.

DON'T BOTHER COMING BACK.

Shaking, I dropped my phone, and the tears were coming.

'Effy? Fucking hell.' Katie got up and danced around me, picking up the phone. 'What's going on? Who was that?'

She looked at the message still open on the screen. Looked back at me.

'Don't you fucking dare gloat,' I told her, wiping my nose with my sleeve.

There was silence as I kept my head down, level with Katie's cork sandals.

'I'm not gloating,' she said quietly. She moved to sit beside me on the step. I was still holding my cigarette, burnt down to its butt. She took it gently from me and stubbed it out on the ground. 'Stuff comes back and bites you on the arse,' I heard her say, although the blood was still pounding in my head. 'I suppose you're meant to learn from it, or some clichéd bollocks like that.'

I looked up, expecting a patronising smile on her baby-doll face. But there was something different there. Pity.

And we can't have that.

I rubbed at my eyes, dryer now. And breathed out slowly. It was five o'clock. A bit early for an aperitif, but fuck it.

'I don't give a toss,' I said. 'He can go fuck himself. They all can.' I checked to see how much money I had. 'Come on,' I told her. 'We're going to get wasted.'

'OK,' said Katie, looking at me warily. 'If that's what you want.'

By nine o'clock I could hardly stand up, and Katie was leaning against the counter of this little bar we were in. It was heaving with people. A chiselled-looking guy in his early twenties was standing looking at me from the other side. He said something to the bloke he was with, and came over.

'*Ciao*,' he said showing all his teeth and ignoring Katie. Scruffy leather jacket and a thin T-shirt so you could see the muscles in his chest. He gestured at my glass, adding in good English, 'Can I buy you a drink?'

'Sure,' I said coolly. 'As many as you like.' Katie giggled. 'And one for my friend here, please.'

'Bossy,' he said, amused, looking me up and down. 'You are always so demanding?'

'You don't ask, you don't get.' I said airily, giving him my glass. 'Excuse us . . . We're just going outside for some additional sustenance.' He raised an eyebrow as I pushed Katie towards the door.

Outside, I clumsily rolled another spliff under one of the tables. An older, well-dressed couple strolling past, arm in arm, looked disdainfully at me and what I was doing.

'Is there a problem?' I asked them loudly. The man shook his head, whispering something to his wife.

'Fuck off then,' I called after them. 'Tossers.'

'Effy,' Katie said, shocked. 'Watch it. You'll get us bloody arrested.'

I patted her arm. 'Effy knows what she's doing.'

Katie didn't exactly look reassured as I lit the spliff. 'I don't—'

But I inhaled as she spoke and had an immediate head rush and nausea. I could feel the sweat on the back of my neck. I held the joint away from me. 'Wow,' I said. 'I think I may be fucked.'

'You don't say,' said Katie, waving away the joint when I offered it to her. 'Let's go back inside.'

I dropped the spliff on the ground and followed her through the doors, where Chisel Face was waiting. He held up two glasses of clear liquid. I grabbed one of them, and sniffed it.

'I hope you haven't put Rohypnol in that,' I said rudely.

Katie looked apologetically at him. 'My name's Katie,' she said, demurely. 'And this is my friend Effy.'

The guy nodded, looking distinctly put off by both of us. No matter.

'Anyway, cheers then,' I said, clinking my glass against his bottle of beer. 'Laters.'

I gripped Katie's arm and led her through the door to the toilets. I had an urgent need to vomit.

As I emerged from the cubicle ten minutes later, Katie was waiting for me, leaning up against the Durex machine.

'Getting some supplies?' I slurred. 'Case you get lucky?'

'No.' Katie handed me a paper towel. 'Wipe your face. You've got sick all over it.'

I snatched it off her and looked in the mirror. My eye make-up had run in ugly rivulets down my face, which was pale and blotchy from the vomiting. A bit of sick was stuck in my hair. I pawed at it with my hand.

'I'll take you home,' said Katie, coming towards me. 'Come on.'

I ignored her, wiping my face with the paper towel.

'Effy,' Katie persisted. She put her hand on my shoulder. 'It probably won't always be this shit.'

I turned and inclined my head, looked at her impassively for a second. 'Well, not for me it won't.'

I watched her expression turn from concerned to confused.

'See, I don't have to try, Katie. Not like you. You'll always have to try. Because . . . well, let's face it, you're not actually all that under your Widow Twanky make-up. And you're really not very bright. You're just . . .' I waved my hand

165

around her face. 'So. Fucking. Pointless.' I stuck my bottom lip out at her, shrugged and chucked the towel into the bin.

Katie looked like I'd slapped her. 'You're really fucking out of it, Eff—'

'Oh, I'm not that out of it,' I hissed. 'Because you're just as sad and cheap and desperate as you are when I'm sober.' I paused, smiled sweetly: 'Might as well fucking kill yourself now 'cause, believe me – and I'm saying this as a friend – no one's ever going to want you.'

Katie moved towards me, her face perfectly composed. 'Whatever makes you feel better, Effy.' She turned to go, but stopped. 'I know you can't fucking stand me seeing you chase after your little crush.' She raised her finger and pointed it at me. 'But most of all, you can't stand it that you might, in any way, shape or fucking form, have *anything* in common with me.' She dropped her hand and opened the door.

'I'll be gone tomorrow,' she said. 'First thing.'

Katie

Venice at night

I left Effy in that bar and kept walking. No bloody clue where I was going. Fuck knows how many of those dolls' house bridges I went over but I came to a halt on one of them, stood leaning over watching a couple in a gondola, arms around each other. The guy guiding the boat looked up at me as he came to the bridge.

166

'*Bella*,' he whispered up into the hot night air.

I smiled, gulping back tears. You haven't seen me without my mask on, I thought. You wouldn't say that if you had.

What a fucking horrible night.

Since the big drama of Aldo's birthday party, the old lady getting carted away in an ambulance and Effy's mum rushing round in a panic, Effy had gone into herself. Totally. I've never spent this much time alone with her, and let me tell you: it was a real fucking eye-opener.

When everyone had gone, all the fizz just evaporated. I wasn't bothered. I'd been a bit bored, trying to talk to some of the neighbours, not having a clue what they were on about.

I'd started necking some of the liqueurs in the living-room cupboard. They tasted rank. I spat the first mouthful into the bathroom sink and checked out my outfit. Not for the first time in this hoity-toity place I felt cheap and nasty. Effy was right about that.

Effy had shut the door on the last guest, looking spaced out. Looking happy, come to think of it. As I was brushing my teeth I did a join-the-dots in my head. When I'd looked over at her earlier, she'd been standing with Aldo. He was unwrapping that present and her face was lit up. She was looking at the guy like he was all her Christmases come at once. I watched him embrace her when he saw what it was, and she nestled her face on his shoulder.

Then Anthea had come rushing in and everything kicked off. Effy just stood there hugging herself, completely useless. As Aldo and her mum got busy telling everyone they had to leave, Effy couldn't take her eyes off him.

Besotted.

I'd wiped my face and turned off the bathroom light. When I walked into the bedroom, Effy was lying star-shaped on the bed, staring up at the ceiling.

'All right?' I sat on the edge and yawned. 'Poor old girl,' I said. 'Florence.'

'Yeah,' said Effy. She shifted her legs over so that I could lie down. 'Shame, because I was beginning to enjoy myself.'

I made a face. 'Yes, how inconvenient of her,' I said. 'To have a funny turn just when you were starting to have a good time.'

Effy looked sharply at me. 'Obviously I care about Flo,' she said defensively. 'I hope she's going to be OK.'

I pursed my lips. 'Course she will,' I said. 'She'd probably been at the sherry.' I paused. 'So, he liked his present, I take it. Aldo?'

'I think so,' she said, too casually.

'He's got a bit of a soft spot for you, I reckon.' I turned to face her, propping my face up on one elbow. 'What do you think?'

Effy didn't answer at first. She pulled the sheet out from under us and wrapped it partially around her. 'Maybe,' she said eventually. 'Who knows?' She switched the bedside light off. 'I'm knackered,' she said, sleepily. 'Try not to snore too loudly tonight.'

'Fucking cheek.' I slid down and turned the other way.

Something was going on. I just hadn't quite figured out what yet.

This morning Anthea was still at the hospital with

168

Florence. She texted Effy to keep her updated. Said she'd be back as soon as the old girl was stable.

'Is Aldo with her d'you think?' I said innocently as we worked our way through a packet of chocolate pastries in the kitchen.

'How should I know?' snapped Effy. She lit a cigarette and opened her mum's guidebook.

We sat around the flat for hours. I suggested going out, but Effy kept saying she wanted to be here. In case Anthea came home early.

Yeah, right.

Effy kept disappearing at ten-minute intervals. The fifth time she came back breathless into the flat, I confronted her in the hallway.

'Training for the marathon?' I asked.

Effy scowled as she pushed past me. 'No . . . just feel restless, that's all.'

'Well let's go out, then,' I said. 'I'm going fucking stir crazy in here.'

She shook her head. 'You go out if you want.'

I sighed and went back into the kitchen for another half-hour of headfuck Italian radio.

Aldo didn't appear. I figured he was busy tending to Florence too.

Effy was like a cooped-up Rottweiler. Snarling at me every time I opened my mouth. Time to leave. It wasn't working out and I kind of missed my own dysfunctional little family.

Then finally, this afternoon, Anthea came home. Aldo was with her.

Effy was scrubbing out some pan that had not in actual fact been used. She was fucking weird.

'Florence is out of danger,' sighed Anthea, sinking into one of the kitchen chairs. 'Poor lady. Her family's miles away.'

Effy didn't answer, just turned the tap to maximum velocity, deafening the rest of us.

Aldo crossed over to the sink and turned it off. 'Your mother is exhausted,' he told her, not unkindly. 'Please. She needs quiet.'

Effy dropped the pan headlong into the soapy water, splattering him.

'She can fucking have it then,' she said, walking out and slamming the kitchen door.

The three of us looked at each other. Aldo rubbed Anthea's shoulder. 'She'll be fine,' he told her. 'She's upset about Florence.'

No she fucking isn't, you idiot, I thought. But I smiled at them.

'I'll go and make sure she's all right. Take her out somewhere,' I said, noticing the shared look of relief between them.

So we ended up walking to another one of those squares and sitting on the steps for an hour. Funny, because I'd actually felt sorry for Effy then. I was on her side.

But as I stared down into that murky water now, the couple in the gondola disappearing out of sight, I felt further away from her than ever.

Even though, in fact, we're just the fucking same.

I got out my phone and texted my mum.

COMING BACK TOMORROW. LOVE YOU.

Katie

Wednesday 19 August

Bordeaux

As the train pulled into the station and I saw Mum in her gold espadrilles, flipping through a copy of *Paris Match*, I felt a surge of affection. For my mum and dad, for James, and for Emily. Specially Emily.

'Yoohoo!' Mum waved her magazine at me. 'Hello, babe.'

I heaved my bag up on my shoulder. 'Hi,' I said, smiling. 'Am I ever glad to see you.'

Mum beamed. 'We've missed you KitKat,' she said, giving me one of her 'warm' hugs – basically a little squeeze of the arm. 'It's just a shame Emily's gone back. She was hoping to see you.'

'Em's gone back?' I said, disappointed.

'Yeah. I'm not pleased, but she's been in a funny mood the last few days. Pining for that girl.'

'Naomi?' I said.

'Yes, Naomi.' Mum sighed. 'Pity. I hoped she and Josh might hit off. Seems like such a nice boy.'

I couldn't help grinning. 'I'm pretty sure he's gay, Mum. Emily told me.' I paused. 'Is she OK?'

'Course she is,' chirped my mother. 'Tough as old boots, us Fitches. She'll get through this phase, then everything will go back to normal.'

'Whatever that is,' I murmured. 'I'm not sure it is a phase. Emily's in love, Mum. It's pointless pretending it isn't happening.'

Mum looked at me sharply. 'You've changed your tune.'

'Well, maybe *I've* changed.' I said.

Mum gave me a curious look. 'You look tired, babe.'

'Yeah.' I dumped my bag in the boot of the car. 'I'm shattered, Mum.'

'So. Apologised has she?' said Mum as we drove back. 'Effy?'

I chewed my lip. 'Let's just say we reached an understanding.'

Mum looked sideways at me. 'That's great. It's horrible when you fall out with your pals, KitKat.'

I gazed out of the passenger window.

God, Mum. You'll never know the half of it.

'Emily's probably on the train back to Bristol now,' Mum went on. 'She left at the crack of dawn this morning.'

'I'll give her a ring,' I said. My stomach fluttering. I had some things I needed to tell my sister.

I walked into the bedroom and saw Emily's bed, neatly made up. Her things gone from the bedside table. Hangers without her clothes in the wardrobe. I dumped my bag on the floor, and sat in the armchair by the window. I tucked my legs underneath me and called her number.

When she answered I could hear the swish of the train, the staticky noise in the background.

'Katie,' she said, sounding flat. 'How's Venice?'

'I'm back at the chalet,' I said quickly. 'Effy and I have parted company.'

'Oh.' There was a brief pause. 'So, want to tell me what the fuck that was all about?' she said. 'Do you know how worried I was when I woke up and you'd just fucking disappeared? And I couldn't even call you, you idiot.' She paused again. 'I can't believe you actually nicked my phone to stop me talking to Naomi. Unfucking-believable.'

I took a breath. 'I'm sorry,' I said. 'I was . . . I felt like you and me . . . Like I'd lost you, for ever.' I shut my eyes, trying to get my words right. 'You and Naomi. I want what you've got so bad. And I was scared that you loved her more than you love me.' I rubbed at my knee. 'Hiding your phone. The things I said. I was out of order. I was jealous. I was trying to hurt you.'

Emily sighed. 'You were a bitch, but I can understand. I've had to stand in your shadow all our lives, remember? And I know I was too wrapped up in my own shit. I didn't have time for yours. But that doesn't mean I don't love you. Naomi's my girlfriend, but who knows what will happen there. You and me. We're stuck with each other.' She gave a short laugh. 'Running to Effy though? That was a fucking curveball.'

'I know. Seemed like a good idea at the time,' I said. 'And to be honest, I'm glad I went.'

'Really?'

'Yeah. I mean, Effy's a fucking fruitloop.' I paused. 'I might be a silly tart sometimes, but at least I'm not that fucked up.'

'No. You're just lonely, and you've been hanging out with the wrong blokes,' said Em. 'You'll find someone, Katie. Someone who's actually worth it.'

'Yeah.' I felt my eyeballs pricking.

'So, what's going on with her, then? Effy?'

'Jesus, there was some weird shit going on with this older bloke. Alfredo. It became pretty obvious that she was after him. As soon as I sussed that out, she turned on me. Really fucking laid into me.'

'What a surprise,' said Emily. 'How old was he then?'

'Forty. Not bad actually. Good-looking. Divorced. Charming, I s'pose.'

'So, nearly killing you in the woods,' said Emily. 'That was all for nothing. She's obviously well over Freddie McClair.'

'Oh, I'm not so sure about that,' I said. 'But fuck knows what goes on in Effy's head. She was low. Like totally on the edge. I feel sorry for her, actually, in a way.'

There was a silence.

'Em? You still there?'

'Still here.'

'I'm so glad you're my sister,' I said happily. 'You're a top twin.'

'Shut up,' said Emily.

'I mean it. I'll never understand why you fancy girls.

But it doesn't matter. You'll always be my special sister.' My voice started breaking up.

'You'll always be my special sister, too,' said Emily. 'Special Needs, that is.'

'Fuck off.'

We lapsed into silence again. I wiped my nose with a tissue. 'So. We friends again?'

'Yeah,' said Emily. 'It'll take more than one of your fucking hissy fits to get rid of me.'

I smiled. 'Thanks,' I said. 'Thank you, Emily.'

There was no reply, her signal had gone. I held on to my phone and sat curled up, looking at the wall.

For the first time in months I felt lucky to be me.

Emily

Wednesday 19 August

Home again

I opened the door before she could knock, and for a second we just stood and looked at each other.

'Hey,' she said, seriously. 'How's it going?'

'Much better now,' I said, my lips longing to kiss the look off her face. 'Now that you're standing in front of me.'

'Really?' Naomi raised an eyebrow. 'I suppose it's good to see you, too.'

'Bitch,' I said, laughing, and reached and grabbed her by her T-shirt. 'You're gonna have to do better than that.'

I pulled her inside and shut the front door. Then I took off my dress, and stood in my bra and knickers. 'Use your imagination,' I told her, tracing around my belly button with my finger. 'You're good at that.'

'I'll see what I can do,' she said softly now, pulling me towards her and leaning in to kiss me.

I closed my eyes and felt her hands skimming over my tits,

then flutter down my tummy and into my knickers. She knelt down.

'Let's take these off you,' she said.

I moaned as she gently parted my legs and started licking me in the way I like – lapping my thighs with her tongue, teasing me until she got to my clit.

'You're doing really well so far,' I told her breathlessly. 'Keep it up.'

We made our way through every room in the house, fucking on the kitchen table, the living-room sofa, in front of the mirror in my parents' room, and in the bathroom, making full and novel use of the shower head, and the various shampoo bottles on offer. By the time we got to mine and Katie's room we were too tired to do anything but hold each other.

We lay in silence for a bit, just being together.

'I love you, girl,' I said.

She kissed the top of my head. 'I missed you like hell,' she whispered into my hair.

'I don't ever want to be apart for that long again,' I said. I raised my head up on my elbow and looked at her. 'Why don't we spend next summer together?'

'Sounds good to me, lover.'

I grinned. 'And I was thinking we could take a gap year and go travelling. Maybe even two years.'

'Do people take two years off before starting uni?' asked Naomi, sleepily.

I lay back down, resting my head on her chest. 'Yeah, 'course. We just apply when we get back.'

I thought about the brochures under my bed for round-the-world trips: South America, Australasia, the US, South East Asia. Maybe even Russia or China. Naomi and I would do it all together. It'd be the kind of experience that binds people forever.

Naomi had fallen asleep, her chest rising and falling rhythmically. Typical. I craned my neck to kiss her gently on the lips, then snuggled into her.

I'd sorted things out with my girls. Nothing else mattered but that.

Pandora

Thursday 20 August

Pandora's bedroom

'Panda?'

Mum tugged at my duvet, but I couldn't move. I was exhausted.

Thommo and I spent hours on Brandon Hill last night, talking and kissing and smoking spliff. We got totally hyperactive in the end, dancing around like crazies, until I got chased by a dog and started screamin'. That's when we got the evils from a few people and had to leave. Neither of us had any money left, 'cause we'd spent it all on spliff and doughnuts and cider, so Thomas gave me a piggy-back to the end of my road, poor boy. He insisted.

'I am strong, Princess Panda. I am a lion.' He roared and whirled me around fast, till we both felt dizzy, then put me down by the postbox.

'Goodnight.' He kissed my hand and then my lips, and he squeezed me tight. 'I will see you tomorrow.'

It must have been gone midnight when I got in.

And Mum would have words today. She knows Effy is on holiday.

She tickled my foot and I started giggling.

'Mummy, stop!' I shot up in bed. My hair was sticking out like a flipping scarecrow, I could see it in the mirror on my dressing table.

Mum picked up my hairbrush from the table and came to sit on my bed.

'Look at you, Panda.' She started brushing my hair, which I love. I crossed my legs over each other and closed my eyes.

'You were very late last night, Panda,' said Mum after a minute. 'Where were you? Effy's away with her mum, isn't she?'

I recognised that tone of voice. Sort of sweet and gentle, but with a cold bit underneath. It seemed like a good time to be honest with Mum – now that I had her undivided attention. But it was important that I chose my words carefully.

'I was out with my new friend Thomas.'

The words kind of hung awkwardly in the air for a bit and I watched her face as it clouded over.

'He's lovely, and kind,' I went on. 'And he doesn't know anyone here, not really.' That bit came out in a bit of a rush. I didn't want to give her time to think up her own image of Thomas. 'He's not what you think.'

'Wait a minute, Pandora . . .' Mum said slowly. 'Why haven't you told me about this boy before?'

'Because you don't want me going out with boys yet. You said so.'

'I didn't say that exactly. I am not happy with you having serious boyfriends, that's all,' she said. 'Boys that will encourage you to do things you are not ready to do.'

She gave me a meaningful look.

'Thomas would never make me do anything,' I told her truthfully. 'And he's from the Congo and he lives in a horrible flat with his mum and his little sisters 'cause they ain't got no money, and he works night and day to pay the rent and put food on the table 'cause he ain't got no dad. He's really polite, and he's ever so funny, too.' I stopped, and took a breath. 'You'd really like him.'

I noticed the cloud had moved away from Mum's face. She was smiling a bit. 'He sounds nice, Panda,' she said. 'Perhaps I could meet him?'

'Ripper!' I leapt out of bed and put my socks on. 'I'll invite him round for tea shall I? Tonight.'

'Tonight?' Mum looked flustered. 'Well, I . . . Tonight?'

'Yeah. I'll ring him straight away and tell him.' I couldn't believe how easy that had been. Maybe it would all be OK after all!

I left Mum still sitting on my bed and ran downstairs to call Thomas.

Thomas turned up at seven wearing a tie and holding flowers.

'You look fucking gorgeous, boy,' I squealed. 'I love your tie.'

He kissed me on the cheek and whispered, 'Oxfam.' The backs of my knees tingled.

Mum came out of the kitchen, her neck covered with the

big red blotches that always come up when she is stressed out. Thomas stuck out his hand and said, 'Mrs Moon. I am so happy to meet you.'

Mum smiled like everyone does when they meet him. 'I'm happy to meet you too, Thomas,' she said.

'These are for you.' He handed her the flowers.

'How lovely.' Mum sneezed and passed them over to me. 'Put these in the green jug, would you Panda? Thomas?' She turned back to him. 'Can I take your jacket?'

I watched them from the kitchen door and gave a little handclap. Thomas saw me and winked while Mum put his coat in the hall cupboard. I went to put the flowers in water.

'Now,' said Mum, coming into the kitchen with Thomas behind her. 'You two go into the living room and watch some TV. I'll bring through some drinks. Homemade lemonade OK for you, Thomas?'

'Very nice, Mrs Moon. Thank you,' Thomas beamed at her.

'Don't worry,' I whispered as we made ourselves comfy on the settee. 'I've got some vodka in a jam jar.'

He grinned. 'Good girl,' he whispered back. 'But your mother is a nice woman.'

The spread of his thigh on the sofa and the feel of it firm against my leg was turning my insides to orange jelly. My favourite.

After dinner of spaghetti carbonara and apple crumble, we all sat in the living room feeling full. But I was getting butterflies too.

Mum always goes to bed at half past ten, so I knew it was getting close to the moment I'd been working up to all evening. She got up from the table and started clearing the dishes, and Thomas jumped up to help.

'Thanks, but there's no need,' said Mum. 'You should be getting home. I didn't realise how late it was.'

'Actually Mum,' I said, 'I was thinking, as it's so late, that um, that maybe Thomas could stay here tonight.' I shut my eyes quickly then opened them again.

Mum's smile had disappeared off her face.

'I don't think so. Thomas needs to get home,' she said over-calm, like. 'It's been a lovely evening.'

She got up and went to the hall cupboard to get his jacket. I think I'd put too much vodka in my lemonade because I felt the fearless feeling coming over me.

'Thomas and I are in love with each other. And I'm nearly eighteen,' I announced like Speedy Gonzalez, knowing it was going to make no difference.

'Panda,' Thomas hissed, pulling me by the arm as I started walking towards her. 'Panda, stop it.'

I shook his hand away. There weren't no turning back.

Mum was walking back into the living room. Her face was like stone.

'Now, Pandora, you are embarrassing me and embarrassing Thomas,' she said with ice in her voice. 'This is my house and I am telling you that you are not having a boy to stay overnight. The same would be true if you were twenty-eight or thirty-eight.'

'It was nice meeting you too, Mrs Moon,' said Thomas, edging out of the room. 'Thank you for a delicious dinner.'

I tried to take his hand as he walked past me, but he wouldn't let me.

'Thomas?' I glared at him.

'Goodbye,' he said, stiffly.

This was not going at all as I'd planned it in my head. Thomas was trying to put his jacket on and open the front door at the same time. He never even looked back at me. And then he was gone.

At this point I wanted to lie down on the carpet and beat my legs against the floor in frustration. But even I knew that wouldn't exactly help my case.

'I'm going to bed,' said my mum. 'I think we should forget this ever happened.'

'I'm not a fucking kid!' I shouted. 'You can't treat me like a baby no more.'

'Pandora, just look at you. You are a child.' Mum sighed. 'You're not ready for . . . for sexual relations yet.'

'Oh yes I am. I've already done it.' I stood looking at her, watched her eyes go enormous.

'You've what?'

'I've already had sex, Mother. It's no big fucking deal.'

'Will you stop swearing!' Mum came towards me and her face was white like a sheet. 'I can't believe what I'm hearing. I am ashamed of you.'

'I'm not a little girl.' I couldn't shut up. 'I'm an adult nearly.'

'You think having sex is what makes you an adult, do you?' Mum came towards me; she was shaking. 'It is not. Any fool can have sex.' She wrapped her cardigan round her, hugging herself. 'It's these girls you hang around with. They are a bad influence.'

'Oh, Mum . . .' I started to cry. 'I know my own mind.

185

It's me who wants it.' I wiped my face. 'You just don't really know me. You're stuck in a flipping time warp. I'm fed up with pretending to be what you want me to be.'

Mum opened her mouth, but no words came out this time. Then there was just the sound of the telly in the living room for a minute, 'cause Mum and I were officially at loggerheads.

'Well,' she said eventually. 'As you say. You're nearly eighteen. If you're so grown up then perhaps you should find somewhere else to live?' She turned to go upstairs. 'Then you can do whatever you want.'

'Mum,' I sobbed. 'Please try and understand?'

'Goodnight Pandora.'. She climbed the stairs and didn't look back at me. 'Please turn the lights off when you leave.'

I stood in the hall for like ten minutes, just starin' at the carpet. I was trembling. 'Course the thing about growing up is taking the consequences of your actions. Mum didn't want me in her house as I was, and I weren't changing. So, there was nothing for it but I had to go. Tonight.

I tiptoed upstairs and got my old school gym bag and stuffed some clothes in and my tootbrush and my phone charger. Then I crept back down and phoned Aunt Lizzie from the living room.

'Of course you can stay here, Panda,' she said. 'For tonight. But you must tell your mother where you've gone.'

'Course I will.'

I angrily wrote a note for Mum, and drew a picture of a sad face while I was at it.

It was time for tough love.

Naomi

Thursday 20 August

Emily's bedroom

Emily flung her arm out across my chest, her lips moving, saying something incomprehensible in her sleep.

I put my hand over hers – small, smooth – and shifted in the bed. It was way too soft. I hadn't slept a wink all night. Not just because we'd woken up every hour to cling to each other, but because my mind had been racing. I was uneasy. I wanted so many things all at once, but it didn't seem possible. Something had to give.

I carefully stretched one leg out of the bed.

'Naomi,' said Emily groggily. I turned to see her, one eye shut, the other trained on me.

'I need some water,' I said quietly, leaning to kiss her on her forehead. She smiled sleepily and turned over.

I walked to the window, looked down on the ring of houses that made up the cul-de-sac. Neatly drawn curtains, gleaming cars in the driveways. Clean and tidy.

I drew back and regarded the windowsill. A ten-year-old Barbie stood to attention in one corner, a cheapo diamante ring swinging from the plastic wrist. Then the multi-coloured My Little Ponies – matted hair, also accessorised with some fucking horrible nylon thongs draped offensively over the ears of one of them. A pink fluffy heart lay on its side – another remnant of Katie's past. Someone had crudely stitched *Happy Valentine's Lover* into the middle. Jesus.

Katie's bed was adorned with cuddly toys, and a discarded nightie – if you can call a strip of satin a nightie. Above her bed a poster of David Beckham in his Armani briefs, a love-heart sticker over his bulging crotch.

The room was like some kind of creepy paedophile shrine. This wasn't a teenager's bedroom. This was a sleepover nest for twelve-year-olds. Fucking immature twelve-year-olds at that.

How could Emily stand it? That tiny bed, waking up to Katie every morning? It was suffocating.

I thought of my own room, which seemed vast in comparison. My big expensive futon that I'd saved up for over a summer working in Topshop on Saturdays. My vintage quilt. My rip-off Starck lamp. And above my bed my new Rothko print.

I went downstairs to get myself some water, and turned the kettle on while I was at it. I'd make us both a cup of tea, then I'd feel more normal.

As I stood waiting for the water to boil, excited thoughts crept back. I'd been so pleased to see Emily yesterday, so fucking relieved to have her back with me. So desperate to touch and explore her body, still new and thrilling. If only we could just stay frozen in this summer. Not have to move forward. Moving forward scared me. I stirred the tea and absently watched a wasp repeatedly headbutt the window. Did *not* moving forward scare me even more?

I took the tea upstairs, and pushed open the bedroom door with my foot. Emily stirred as I came in, saw the tea and pushed herself up on her pillow. She smiled contentedly, looking fresh-faced and gorgeous.

'This bed is fucking ridiculous, Em,' I said, putting the mugs down on the table next to it. 'My feet were hanging over the edge all night.'

'Sorry, babe.' She sipped her drink. 'I suppose we could have gone into Mum and Dad's.' She laughed at my horrified face. 'But I didn't think you'd be up for that somehow.'

I grinned. 'You thought right.' I lay back next to her, stroking her free arm with my fingertip. 'It wasn't that bad. My toes were cold, is all.'

She smiled happily. 'Thank fuck that holiday's over,' she said, sounding more awake. 'I couldn't wait to see you.'

'Likewise,' I said. 'It was torture.'

'But now it's done,' she said, happily. 'From now on, wherever you go, I go.' She slurped some more tea. 'And vice versa.'

I thought of Kieran, and of what we'd talked about. I winced. I didn't want to think about that now, but it wouldn't go away. I shook my head, feeling muddled.

'There are so many things out there for us,' Emily went on. She put her empty mug back on the table. 'For us to do together. Before uni, and work, and responsibility.' She closed her eyes. 'Can't wait.'

I smiled uneasily. 'One day at a time, Em,' I said. 'Let's enjoy it as it comes.' I paused. 'I'd better get back soonish – Mum asked me to go to the garden centre with her and help her carry back some more triffids.'

As I spoke, I could feel Emily's hurt, even though I couldn't see it. I looked down at her. She smiled, uncertainly, but snuggled against me.

'Don't go yet, babe,' she said, quietly. 'Stay a bit longer.'

I put my arms around her and held her tightly, kissing her nose. 'OK,' I said, 'I'll stay a bit longer.'

Pandora

Friday 21 August

Aunt Lizzie's house, Bristol

'Panda, dear,' said Aunt Lizzie, pouring us both a cup of tea and passing me the Jammy Dodgers. 'Are you sure Angela is happy with you staying here?'

I put a whole biscuit into my mouth. Usually I like to take the top layer of biscuit off and eat the jam first, but I've not been myself lately. I swallowed.

'Mum and I are goin' through a bad patch,' I said. 'She needs teaching a lesson, Aunt Lizzie.'

She raised an eyebrow and took a sip of Earl Grey. 'Does she, dear? What lesson is that exactly?'

'Well.' I eyed the biscuits, wondering about another one. 'She's got to see that I ain't just her little girl that she can push around no more.' I gave in and took another Dodger.

Aunt Lizzie looked like something was tickling her. 'But you'll always be that. Her little girl.' She leaned back and held her cup and saucer in both hands. 'It's not easy for her.'

I frowned. 'What about me, though? Me, standing on the cusp of adulthood,' I said, repeating something I'd read in one of my PSE Guidance books at school. 'It's important for her to respect me with, like, boundaries and stuff.'

'Boundaries, eh?' Aunt Lizzie smiled fondly at me. I love her to bits. I wished she was my mum. 'Whose boundaries?'

'Mine, I s'pose.' I finished the second biscuit, still feeling like I wanted the whole flipping packet. I wasn't sure exactly what I was talking about to be honest, but it sounded right. 'I want her to see that I'm a woman, with the need for privacy and respect.'

'What about your mum needing respect?' said Aunt Lizzie, narrowing her eyes. 'You, respecting her.'

I looked at her. 'What?'

'I mean, my dear,' she said patiently, 'that your mother needs respect. For bringing you up, for looking out for you, for being worried about you.'

'She just don't want me ever to leave home,' I said. 'If she had her way, I'd be following her round Tesco till I'm flipping thirty.' I shook my head. 'And that ain't gonna happen.'

'I think you're hurting her, with what you're doing.'

'She's hurting me,' I said stubbornly. 'I am hurt.'

'Because she doesn't want you to leap into the naughty stuff with Thomas?'

'Well. Yeah. Because of that.'

'Why is that so important to you?'

I was beginning to feel frustrated. 'I thought you were on my side?'

'Now Panda,' said Aunt Lizzie, putting down her cup.

'That response tells me that your mother has a point. If nothing else.'

I closed my eyes. If I was the Incredible Hulk I would be at stage two of the transformation now. My body would be squeezing against my clothes.

I stood up. As I said, I love Aunt Lizzie and I didn't want to cause a scene.

'I'm going for a walk now,' I told her. 'Tea was scrumptious. Thanks.'

I walked out of the living room and went to sit out in the garden on my favourite bench. I looked up at the sky. Blue all the way. I felt lonely. And horny. And confused.

I called Thomas. He was on his tea break from work. He hadn't spoken to me since I'd got here, and I hadn't rung him neither. But now the whole point of me running away was getting a bit muddled in my head.

'Thomas,' I whispered.

'Pandora?' Thomas sounded cautious. 'What is it?'

'I miss you, babycakes.' I closed my eyes. 'I'm sorry about the other night,' I added. 'I did it for us, though. You understand?'

He sighed. 'No, Pandora. I don't think I do.'

'But we need respect as a couple,' I said.

'What do you mean?'

'We need to do what couples do.'

Thomas sighed more deeply. 'And what is that? Have fun together? Be kind to each other? Kiss each other?'

I smiled, a warm oozy feeling coming over me. 'Yes. Loads and loads of kissing. And touching and—'

'Pandora,' said Thommo firmly. 'I am at work.'

193

'You want to do it with me, don't you?' I said, a bit scared now. 'You still want to?'

'At some point, yes,' he said, sounding kind of cold. 'But not to prove a point. And not if it upsets your mother.'

'You care about her more than you care about me,' I said, starting to cry. 'Why is she so important?'

Aunt Lizzie's gardener, working on the box hedge further down the garden, looked up at me as I raised my voice.

'All right.' I calmed myself down. 'I understand. But will you come over? Please.'

There was a silence. 'OK. Tonight, I will come and see you. But to talk, yes?'

'Yes!' I said. 'Come after work – at six?'

I ended the call and held the phone against me. Thomas wouldn't be able to resist me when he saw me. He'd see that resistance is futile.

Another line I'd nicked off some book or another. But it said everything.

Thomas

En route to Aunt Lizzie's, later

I travelled to see Pandora with a heavy heart. To use an excellent English phrase, she was beginning to sound like a broken record.

To me she is beautiful, and pure. There is no side to Panda. Coming from where I do, this is of huge value. I was angry

194

with Cook – for placing this distorted idea into her head that she is simply a willing body for men. My conversation with JJ the other morning has opened my eyes to that one. Not that I am happy with what happened. But perhaps there is a truth in the saying: 'whatever gets you through the night.'

If I am being totally honest though, part of my resistance to Panda and I consummating our relationship is that I feel some distaste that Cook has been there first. This, along with Pandora's persistent obsession is not helping me get in the mood. I would like to have a whole conversation without mentioning sex. I would like Panda to see what she is doing. I am becoming increasingly doubtful that this will happen.

I arrived at just after six. Aunt Lizzie was very pleased to see me and gave me a big, warm hug. She looked warily at Pandora, who was hopping from foot to foot behind her.

'I'm going to give you some space,' she told her. 'But I won't be far away.' She winked at me.

I hardly had time to take my coat off before Pandora rushed at me and embraced me. She pressed her hands on my body, then stroked up and down my back. I very much wanted to reciprocate, it was so good to feel her close to me again, but I resisted. I gently pushed her away.

'Let's sit down,' I said, pointing at the sofa. 'Come on.'

She nestled up to me, and I put one arm around her.

'So glad to see you,' she whispered into my chest. 'Been thinking about you loads.'

'Me too,' I said, stroking her hand. 'This is hard for me.'

She sat up. 'That stupid cow. Stopping us from acting on our urges.' She stabbed at a cushion. 'So bloody childish.'

My mouth fell open. 'Your mother is childish?'

'Well, yeah. I'd say it's pretty immature to want your daughter to be a kid, like, for ever.'

I laughed, though not in amusement. 'My God, Pandora. You have no clue.'

She looked at me, puzzled.

'You are the one who is acting like a child,' I said quietly. 'So desperate for us to have sex.' I rubbed my thighs with my palms, then stopped as I noticed her eyes hungrily following the movement. 'We are more than that. Or so I thought. I'm not so sure now.'

'What the fuck is wrong with you?' she said. She got up and started pacing the living room. 'Boys always want sex. It's normal.'

'Certain boys, perhaps,' I said coldly. 'Not me. Not now.'

She looked at me. 'What do you mean, not now?'

'Not with a girl who prizes this act above all else.' I stood up, and went to pick up my coat. 'I thought better of this girl.'

'Thomas, no.' said Panda. 'Please don't go.'

She began to cry but I already had the front door open. 'Goodbye,' I called to Aunt Lizzie, who had been hovering in the hallway. 'It has been lovely to know you.

'Goodbye Panda,' I said before I closed the door behind me. 'Please take care of yourself.'

Pandora

In bed, later still

I couldn't eat any fish pie that night. Normally it's my favourite. I went to bed at nine o'clock with Edgar, my furry panda, and lay staring at the moon through a gap in the curtains.

At ten o'clock I turned on the light and listened to Girls Aloud on my iPod.

At ten-thirty, I picked up my phone and looked at the pictures I had taken of Thomas. I thought about all the fun we had just messing about on Brandon Hill. All the cuddles and the kisses. The way he listens to everything I say without making me feel like a twat, unlike most people.

At eleven, I texted Effy. She texted back. DON'T BE A TIT.

I thought about how Thomas has changed my life. I don't ever want to go back to before.

I thought about my mum, and her face full of worry and hurt.

Aunt Lizzie was right. I'm a silly, silly girl.

At eleven-thirty, I held my breath and pressed down on his number.

After a long time, he answered. I could hear the sound of the TV in the background.

'Hello?'

'I've been stupid, Thommo,' I whispered into the phone. 'Really childish.'

Thomas didn't answer. I carried on. I had nothing to lose.

'Aunt Lizzie said something about respect today. She said I wasn't respecting my mum.' I swallowed. 'But I'm not respecting you, neither. Am I? What you want?' I closed my eyes.

'That is true,' said Thomas finally. 'But Panda, surely you see that mostly you are not respecting yourself.' He paused. 'I think you don't trust me to love you without offering sex to me. You don't believe that you have anything else.'

I thought of Cook. 'Maybe,' I said.

'But you do. For me. There are a thousand reasons for me to love you.'

'Thomas.' I started crying. 'I'm going home to Mum. I'm going to apologise.'

'Wait there,' said Thomas. He hung up.

At midnight, I looked at my bed, strewn with toilet roll, when there was a tap on the door. 'Night, Aunt Lizzie,' I said, willing her not to come in.

But the door opened, and there was Thomas. He came towards the bed, and pushed all the tissue off on to the floor.

'Can I hold you, Pandora?' he said, taking his trainers off. Then his T-shirt, and finally his jeans.

I nodded and moved over in the bed. He got in, and held me tight, then he kissed my neck. I stroked his back. And then I felt his hands gently pushing up my T-shirt and kissing my tummy. I held my breath and just kept stroking while his tongue moved further up and he nuzzled my boobs.

'Please will you take off your pyjamas, Panda?' he said softly. 'For me.'

198

Effy

Saturday 22 August

Florence's apartment

'Is that you, Anthea?'

'No, Florence,' I said cautiously. 'It's me, Effy.'

I heard bedclothes being thumped about.

'Effy! How lovely. Come in, come in. Door's open.'

I opened the door. Florence was lying on a huge bed facing me. The shutters were part closed, and the room was dimly lit from her bedside lamp.

Florence tried to sit up.

'Don't move,' I said, looking with alarm at her face. One side had dropped slightly, the corner of her mouth tilted down. She put her hand across it, like she was hiding it.

I felt a lurch of fear. It was like when I'd visited Dad's mum in her nursing home when I was about eight. Florence looked so tiny and frail.

'Don't be frightened, girl,' she said. Pulling her bedclothes up a bit. 'This damn stroke has just made me look ancient all of a sudden.' She laughed, with a bit of an effort.

I came forward and perched on the side of the bed. Florence looked at me. Her gaze direct as ever. 'Well,' she said. 'How are you? Anthea said you had a friend to visit. I'm sorry I didn't meet her. Did you have fun?'

I couldn't answer at first. God. Loneliness swamped me. And guilt. Guilt for being such an alpha bloody bitch to Katie. And for sitting here, healthy, with a sick old woman who didn't seem to have a miserable or spiteful bone in her body. I'd say I was humbled. Humbled. Now that's a fucking stranger to my vocabulary if ever there was one.

'Yeah,' I said at last. 'It was OK.'

Florence looked quizzically at me. 'And how's everything else?' she asked. 'Have you seen anything of Aldo lately?'

I was glad of the bedside light. I could feel my face going up in flames. 'A bit,' I said carefully. 'At his party and stuff.'

'He's a good man,' she said wistfully. 'He and your mother. They've been wonderful these past few days.'

'Have they?' My stomach muscles were clenching and unclenching. 'Has he been spending a lot of time with you then?'

'They both have,' she said. 'Quite a double act, those two.' She leaned forward. 'Your mother's a bossy one, isn't she? Had him cleaning the bathroom all yesterday afternoon.' She sat back, and recovered her breath. 'I don't think he's used to that. His ex-wife was a bit of a pushover.'

'How d'you mean?' I asked, not sure I wanted to know.

'Oh, well . . . Apparently she was rather a passive woman. Docile, even. Which made it all much more of a shock when it happened.'

'When what happened?'

'When she announced she'd fallen in love with someone else.' Florence shook her head. 'He was devastated.'

'Poor Aldo,' I said. Half meaning it.

'Yes, Poor Aldo,' she said. 'But, then . . . you never know what's round the corner, do you?' She twinkled at me.

'No,' I smiled, understanding. 'You don't.'

Hope was flaring inside me.

'Love can come from the most unexpected encounters,' she went on. 'In the most inappropriate situations too.' She sighed. 'Of course, that's all behind me. More's the pity. I have to be happy with living it vicariously.'

'I don't know about that, Flo.' I looked around at the bed and nudged her leg. 'I bet you could fit a few more in here.'

'Naughty!' Flo batted playfully at me. 'I must admit, I wouldn't mind one last turn round the dancefloor, Effy. Just a short waltz.' She paused. 'If you know what I mean?'

'Got a pretty good idea, yes,' I said laughing, wondering at how she had managed to wipe my loneliness away so quickly. Because inside I was doing my own dance. Of total fucking jubilation.

All that frustration. Like a caged animal for days. And now this.

Florence's eyelids were starting to droop a little. 'Oh, I am tired,' she murmured. 'All this love in the air. It's doing me in.'

I shifted off the bed. 'I'll leave you to sleep, Flo,' I said. 'I'll come back tomorrow.'

'Effy,' she said, suddenly gripping my hand. 'It's all part of life, you know.'

201

'What is?'

'Loving, and losing,' she said, her eyelids drooping. 'Accepting what is meant to be.' She smiled dozily and wafted her hand in the air. 'Etcetera.'

I nodded. 'I think I know what you mean.'

I left Florence dropping off to sleep and practically skipped up to our apartment. Mum was cooking something, singing to herself in the kitchen.

Grin and bear it, I told myself. You can afford to be generous.

'Hello,' she said. 'How was Florence?'

'Great,' I said, sitting down. 'I really like her.'

'She's a crafty old bird,' said Mum, who was not looking unattractive. Or maybe it was the heat from the cooker? Whatever, it was good she was happy. I was happy. We were all fucking happy.

'Yeah, she's wise, I reckon.' I took a handful of grated parmesan and crammed it in my mouth. It was then I noticed that the table was set for three.

'Who's coming for dinner?' I asked, knowing.

Mum tested the pasta with a fork. 'Alfredo,' she said lightly. 'Poor bloke's been doing Florence's odd jobs for her lately. He'll waste away if I don't feed him.'

If only you could feed him and then piss off and leave us alone, I thought.

'I could have cooked something.' I was on the verge of sulky.

'That's sweet,' she said absently. 'But it's probably quicker . . . and tidier . . . if I do it.'

'Well, I'll get some wine,' I said.

'No need.' She drained the pasta. 'Everything's organized. You just sit there and relax.'

Like a powerless child.

'You are fucking bossy, aren't you,' I said, a bit too sharply. But she didn't notice. Too busy mixing her fucking sauce into her fucking pasta.

I poured some wine out and had drunk half of my glass when he knocked on the door.

'Hello,' he said when I opened it, kissing me on both cheeks. 'I'm very glad you are here, eating with us.'

'Me, too.' I leant against the door frame, partly blocking his way.

'I bought some excellent wine.' He held up the bottle and leaned in closer. 'I think we deserve to get very drunk on good wine,' he said. 'Don't you?'

'Yes,' I said, excitement rising. I wanted to kiss the face off him. 'Definitely.'

'Here's to us,' said Mum later, clinking glasses with me and Aldo. 'Here's to a new start.' She looked from me to Aldo. 'For all of us.'

'Absolutely,' said Aldo, looking at me. 'For all of us.'

I gulped down my wine, feeling euphoric. I could hardly believe it, but I was allowing myself to fall in love and I was being rewarded.

'I'm going to skin up,' I said. 'If that's OK?'

We'd finished eating. Mum had fussed about making coffee, while Aldo lamely offered to do the dishes.

'You've spent all morning fixing Florence's plumbing,' she told him. 'Just bloody sit down, would you?'

'Yes, *Signora*,' said Aldo seriously. He winked at me.

It wasn't exactly the vibe I would have wanted – a cosy little family dinner – but it was a start. I looked at him through my eyelashes. I had rolled a joint, and lit it from one of Mum's naff candles. I took a drag, inhaled and passed it to Aldo.

'Effy . . .' he said, shaking his head. 'You are leading me astray.'

'Yes,' said Mum, pouring coffee into tiny cups. 'Effy's good at that.'

'Whereas you're Snow fucking White,' I said, taking back the spliff. 'A lovely, caring Mummy.'

Mum glanced at me, narrowing her eyes. 'You're destroying your brain cells,' she said, gesturing at the spliff in my hand. 'You'll wake up a bloody vegetable one day.'

'What, you mean like a potato?' I said, childishly. 'Or a Brussels sprout?'

Mum rolled her eyes. 'For some people it doesn't take so long,' she said. 'You might be one of them.'

'Ah, now Effy is clearly very bright,' said Aldo. 'As well as beautiful.'

I felt my head rocking from side to side. 'That's good,' I said. 'Because beauty is not enough.' I smiled at him. It seemed as though he was moving away from me. I looked down at the joint and then waved it in his direction. 'Is it?'

A flicker of discomfort touched his expression. He took the spliff from me and stubbed it out. 'Are you OK?' he asked, his voice retreating now. I heard Mum saying something but I couldn't make out the words. I scraped my chair back.

'Need to go to the Ladies,' I said, getting up. I wanted to

pass out. Fuck, the wine, or the weed, was way too strong. I attempted a sober exit, but crashed into Aldo's chair.

'Steady,' he said, his hand on my waist. I stayed still, enjoying the feel of his long fingers straddling my hip.

'Will you help me to the loo?' I said, putting my hand over his. 'I think I am a little worse for wear.'

'Take her,' said Mum, sounding peeved. 'Or she'll crack her head open on the basin.'

'You can come in with me if you like,' I whispered unsteadily as we got to the bathroom door. 'You can help me take my knickers down.'

Aldo laughed, a short nervous laugh. I leaned back on the door, and pulled his arm towards me.

'Come on,' I said. 'Don't tell me you haven't thought about it.'

He dropped his arm to take my hand. 'You are a lovely, but very confused girl,' he said quietly.

'I'm not confused,' I said. 'I know exactly what's going on.'

'Effy.' He clasped my hand tighter. 'Please. Don't do this.'

'OK,' I nodded solemnly. 'I'll be a good girl. I promise. For you.'

He let go and brushed his hand through his hair. 'I'll say good night,' he said. 'I am very tired. I'll see you tomorrow. OK?'

'Yes,' I whispered, watching him walk back across the hall to the kitchen. 'See you tomorrow.'

When I came out of the bathroom, there was just the sound of Mum clattering pans in the kitchen.

'Goodnight, Mum,' I said. 'I'm going to bed.'

There was a pause, then her voice, thickly.
'Night, Effy,' she called. 'Sleep tight.'

Effy

Sunday 23 August

Via San Angelo, morning

'Oh Dio, il mio amore, mio amore.'

My hand hovered over the handle to her bedroom door, confusion turning to stone-cold horror as I heard his voice and finally realised the truth.

His voice. Their breathing.

I'd woken early, seen the light under her door on my way to the bathroom and stopped to see if she was all right.

I moved quickly back to my room, suddenly the most important thing in the whole world being that they didn't know I was there. I sat on the edge of my bed, shock making me wide-eyed and breathless. I should have fucking seen it coming. What the fuck did I expect from her? Sly bitch. Grabbing whatever she wants. Doesn't matter who gets fucked over in the process. Humiliation and grief swept over me like a black cloak. I covered my mouth with both hands and wailed soundlessly, the effort of making no noise dragging at my throat until it was raw.

Eventually I crawled back into bed. It was still early. I lay for a while, listening in a kind of curdled fascination to the two of them fucking. I must be really twisted because a part of me felt turned on. Not by her, but by the sound of him doing it to her. But the bigger part felt disgusted.

It's not real. It can't be real.

I woke up later to find the door to my bedroom wide open. Someone was pushing a broom around the marble tiles in the hall. Her. She stopped outside my room. I pulled the sheet higher and closed my eyes so I wouldn't have to look at her. Deceitful bitch.

'Effy? You awake?'

I clenched my fists under the sheet and willed her to fuck off, but she came in and sat on my bed.

'Effy love, you need to wake up. I have bad news.'

You don't fucking say.

'It's about Florence.'

I opened my eyes at that, although I still couldn't bring myself to look at her. Mum stroked my shoulder.

'She's dead. Alfredo went to see her this morning and found her.' Her voice broke. 'She died in her sleep.'

I said nothing. Stared at the wall.

'Effy, did you hear me?'

'Yes,' I said, expressionlessly.

Mum kept her hand on my shoulder for a few seconds, but then took it off. In my peripheral vision I could see her bow her head. She knew, then. She knew that I knew.

'Love, I . . .'

'Go away.'

'But . . .'

I turned to the wall, my body tense. 'Please, just fucking leave me alone,' I said, monotone. 'I have nothing to say to you. Now or ever.'

I felt Mum stand up then. Heard her leave the room, shutting the door behind her. And I let the tears come. For Aldo. For Florence. But mostly for me.

I fell asleep again and when I awoke, the apartment was empty. Good. I got dressed. Shortest denim cut-offs, vest. And my boots. I wet my hair and scrubbed it with my hands so it looked wild. Wild child. I should be on my way out to meet some fit Italian kid. Someone my own age.

Don't think about it.

I was looking for my keys when I heard the door to the apartment open. Shit, I'd wanted to be gone by the time she got back.

'Effy? You OK?'

It was him. He had a linen suit on, dark blue shirt. A brown paper bag in his arms. He looked knackered. He walked through to the kitchen and started unpacking the bag. Thick bread, a container of olives, some cheese and ham in greaseproof paper. A bottle of wine. He screwed up the bag and left it in the fruitbowl. His eyes flickered over my shorts.

I found my keys behind the sink. 'I'm going out,' I told him, quietly. 'You and Mum can have your lunch in peace.'

'Anthea is down in Florence's apartment . . .' he said, looking lost. And disappointed. 'I had hoped we could have lunch together.' He paused, cleared his throat. 'We could have a talk. I got some very nice wine.' He smiled sadly. 'Please?'

I hesitated because despite everything, I wanted to. I still wanted him. Wanted that pathetic split second of electricity as his fingers brushed mine when he passed me a drink. But the sense of anticlimax, of disappointment, was massive.

'Sorry. You should have said something earlier,' I said. 'I've got plans.'

'Plans?' he said, raising a smile.

Sorry, can't afford to feel sorry for you. Not now.

'Yep.' I jangled the keys restlessly. 'Plans.'

'Of course,' he said. 'The food will be here when you return.'

'Great.' I turned and walked out to the front door, closing it behind me quietly.

Outside I paused at the top of the stairwell, hearing the sounds coming from Florence's apartment. Mum's voice. Furniture being moved. I felt exhausted, and numb.

Dazed, I went out through the lobby and kept on going, eventually finding myself inside Santa Maria. Aldo's church. Whatever, I needed calm, and silence. I ducked into a wooden booth, wanting to block everything out.

A voice spoke in my ear, scaring the fuck out of me. I was in a confessional. A priest's bowed head was visible through a grid to my right. Just like in films. 'I'm sorry,' I whispered. 'I can't speak Italian.'

I saw the priest nod his head. 'Is OK,' he said. 'You stay. God will listen.'

His kindness acted like a tap to my grief, and I started

to sob. 'I don't want to talk,' I managed to say. 'Can I stay anyway?'

The priest nodded again.

So we sat, me and the priest. Him silent on his side, me crying not at all silently on my side, hardly able to breathe with the scale of this . . . catastrophe. This fucking awful, awful catastrophe. Aldo loves my mum. He doesn't love me. He loves my mum. My *mum*. And lovely, kind, understanding Florence is dead and I'll never be able to talk to her again. I groaned, bending over in physical pain as I suddenly understood what she'd really meant when I'd spoken to her, fuck, only a few hours before. Oh God and *Freddie*. I hadn't let myself think about him, and now he didn't want me either. I caught my breath in panic.

I was totally alone. I was roadkill.

The priest spoke again, asked if he could help. I said no and left the booth. I found an empty side chapel and sat down, suddenly exhausted. Feeling heavy, like I was moving under water, I bent to pick up a kneeling cushion. I lay down along the pew, with my head on the cushion; just lay.

After twenty minutes the discomfort got me up and out of there. I started walking home, not knowing what else to do, the grief turning to anger with every step. I began to walk faster and then to run. I just kept running back to the flats, then two steps at a time up to our apartment, panting, growling like a fucking wild animal.

When I burst through the open door to find Mum and Aldo sitting at the kitchen table drinking wine as if nothing was wrong, I didn't stop; I cleared the table with one violent sweep of my arm. Watching glasses and bottle crash to the floor, red wine splattering the cupboards and Mum's T-shirt.

I pointed at her. 'Mucky pup.' I laughed hysterically. 'Mucky bitch.'

'Effy.' She looked frightened, her eyes darting to Aldo. She got up, edged her way round the table, her flipflops crunching over the glass. 'Effy, darling. Please . . .'

'Don't you dare come any fucking closer,' I warned her, shaking. I kicked at the glass, scattering it further around the kitchen. I looked at her: timid eyes, flushed cheeks, mouth kissed all night by him. A sound like a fire alarm seemed to be going off in my head, a relentless noise, pushing me closer and closer to the edge of this.

'You fucking disgust me!' I screamed.

And then I just carried on screaming, not even words, just making noise. I think I fell to my knees, because I was aware of Mum trying to lift me up.

'Leave me, I just want to die,' I wailed, looking down at my knees, bloody from the glass.

She backed away and Aldo took over. I turned on him, thumping him as hard as I could, screaming, until finally he let go and I lay still, spent.

There was nothing left for me.

Week Four

Cook

Monday 24 August

Grapes & Favour bar

'What the fuck are we doing in here?' said Freddie, looking around the place.

'What's wrong with it?' I parked myself on a high stool. 'It's clean, it smells nice . . .' I craned around to see the blackboard behind me. 'And they do a nice pan-fried salmon with lime and coriander mash, Fred. What's not to like?'

He sniffed. 'It's for girls.'

I grinned. 'Precisely,' I said. 'And there's a club night kicking off in about two hours' time. A few beers, a few of Cookie's long lingering looks, and Camilla and Henrietta Posh over there will be putty in our hands.'

'I don't think the "ladies" in here are going to go for your ape-man act somehow,' Freddie said, smirking. He looked over at a couple of girls in pencil skirts and blouses. 'They're a bit too mature.'

'I'm up for the older woman, mate,' I said, rubbing my

hands together. 'I've often wondered about Effy's mum . . . you know . . . in the sack.'

'You're a sick twat,' he said, digging around for money in his pocket. 'But while we're here, we may as well get fuelled up.' He drew out two tenners. 'Usual?'

'Good one,' I said, slapping him on the shoulder. 'And get us some olives while you're at it, there's a love.' I puckered my lips and blew him a kiss.

Freddie rolled his eyes and sauntered over to the bar. I turned to see JJ rocking like a mentalist on his stool.

'What the fuck are you doing, JJ?'

'Trying to pull my chair in to the table, what does it look like?' he said. 'It's not easy when your feet don't reach the floor.'

'Nobody's feet fucking reach the floor, mate,' I said. 'You're supposed to put your feet on the rungs.'

'Right. Yes. I see.' JJ adjusted his feet, and gazed around him.

'Why are they all wearing suits?' he said, just as Freddie returned with our beer. No olives, though. Tight-arse.

'That'll be us in a few years,' said Freddie, plonking the drinks on the table. He placed a lime and soda in front of JJ and patted him on the shoulder. 'Selling our souls for a fucking mortgage or whatever.'

'Speak for yourself,' I said. 'I'm never wearing a fucking suit.'

'Apart from when you're up in court, of course.' Freddie smiled smugly into his bottle. 'Which, let's face it, is only a matter of time.'

I ignored him and looked around the place. Shiny hair

and blouses everywhere, all caning the fucking white wine. What is it with birds and white wine? I leaned over to speak to the next table. Three of them. Perfect.

'Hello ladies, how's it going?'

One of them, dark hair and nips showing through her top, looked me up and down. 'Fine, thanks,' she said, all bored like, and turned back to her friends. Frosty bitch.

'So are you horny or just cold?' I asked, nodding at her tits.

She wasn't impressed with that. Looked at me like I was a piece of shit. I shrugged.

'What?' I said, turning to see Fred's face.

He shook his head. 'Unbelieveable.'

'I know. No fucking sense of humour.'

'That's not what I meant.'

No shit.

'Come on lads,' I said, puffing my chest out. 'Put some fucking welly into it.'

Freddie drank his San Miguel and shrugged, while JJ embarked on some origami shit with the cocktail menu.

'I think you may have to move on,' JJ said. 'Those three girls seem distinctly immune to your charms.' He dropped his head back down, folding like his little life depended on it.

'After a few drinks they'll be gagging for it,' I said, beginning to feel pissed off. I grabbed his paper fucking swan and chucked it on the floor. He gave me one of his hurt looks and started on another.

'Wow, that's amazing!'

Two birds about our age stopped to watch JJ's handiwork. He smiled at them but said nothing, the clueless fucker.

'Yeah, he's good with his fingers is JJ,' I said, winking at the short, cute one.

She ignored me. 'What else can you make?' she asked JJ.

'Only a few, I'm afraid,' said JJ. 'I'm just learning . . . I can do a jumping frog, though.'

The taller one with lips designed to wrap round my cock clapped her hands. 'I love frogs!'

'I'll make one for you,' said JJ. 'I mean, if you like.'

She smiled at him. 'Thanks, I'd love that.'

Freddie and I looked at each other. What the fuck?

'We're going to a new club night later,' I said to the short one. 'Fancy it?' I waggled my eyebrows at her.

'No thank you,' she said, barely looking at me. Too fucking fascinated with what JJ was doing.

He finished and held up his creation. 'At any vertex the number of valley and mountain folds always differs by two in either direction,' he said, grinning at them both. 'Mathematics of paper folding.' He handed the tall one her frog. 'Or of course you can just think of it as a nice way to pass the time.'

I grabbed my bottle, took a swig and belched heartily. The taller girl wrinkled her nose in disgust. 'Pig,' she muttered to her friend.

'You need a new act, Cook,' said Freddie, his lips twitching. 'I don't think the burping Neanderthal is doing it for the clientèle.'

Freddie

After half an hour of watching Cook make a tit of himself and JJ existing in some parallel universe where origami is sexy, my mind started wandering. It wasn't worth falling out with my best friend over a girl. I still felt like punching him in the face every time I thought about him with her, but fuck it, she was bad news. She'd fucked him over too.

I circled the top of my bottle with my finger, trying not to think about college. I hadn't told Cook about the message I'd sent Effy. Telling her not to come back. I'd regretted doing it the moment I'd fucking sent it. The thought of not seeing her again was just . . . shit. I'd missed her. But if she came back the whole bloody thing would start up again. Fuck only knows what she'd been thinking . . . and doing for the past few weeks. I shook my head and drained my three-pound-fucking-fifty bottle of beer.

'What's up with you?' asked Cook, coming back from the bar and seeing my face.

'Nothing.'

He thumped my back. 'Well gis a smile, then.'

'What are you so happy about, anyway?' I asked, nodding towards JJ, still merrily chatting away with his little fan club. 'Even he's doing better than you.'

'A fluke, my friend . . . Anyway, you should know by now that the Cookie Monster doesn't let rejection get him down.'

I looked sideways at him. 'Bollocks.'

Cook attempted a grin, but his eyes were dead. 'Seriously,' he said. 'I'm not bothered no more. She had her chance and

219

she's fucking blown it.' He held up his bottle, and clinked mine. 'With both of us.'

'What about next week?' I said. 'She'll be there. Probably.'

'You reckon?' said Cook. 'I think she's fucked off for good.'

I wiped my hand over my face. Jesus. What a fucking mess. 'Yeah, you're probably right,' I said.

Cook downed a shot. 'Anyway, she doesn't give a shit about either of us, we know that much. All that "Don't contact me in Venice" wank.'

I looked up at him, all front, eyes darting round the room, ready to home in on the next fit girl that walked through the door. Suddenly I felt like grabbing him and holding him. I didn't obviously, because that would be totally fucking gay.

'Yeah,' I said. 'Forget her.'

'That's the spirit, mate,' he said, belting me playfully on the back. 'Now, let's go outside for a smoke?'

JJ

'My name's Sophie,' said the shorter blonde girl. 'And this is Imogen.'

I blushed, utterly astounded by this introduction. I willed myself not to vibrate. 'JJ,' I said, awkwardly sticking my hand out in their direction. 'Well, Jeramiah, actually, but my friends call me JJ. As an abbreviated form of both my Christian name and my surname—'

I stopped, seeing their eyes open wide with the standard freaked-out reaction that I have become accustomed to.

'But that's er . . . boring,' I said. 'You don't want to know that.' I gave a laugh embarrassingly like a girl's and fiddled nervously with the paper frog.

Incredibly, Sophie smiled at me in a friendly way. 'Those your mates, then?' she said, gesturing at Cook and Freddie who were walking outside for a smoke.

'Yes,' I said. 'They are my best friends.'

'Really?' said Imogen. 'Don't you find them a bit of a hindrance?'

The accurate answer to this question would have been undeniably 'Yes.' But this was no time for accuracy. 'They're OK,' I said. 'They're just forthright.'

'That's one word for it, I suppose,' said Sophie, wrinkling her rather pretty nose. 'But the fair one? He's a total cock.'

'Cook actually,' I said. 'His name is Cook.'

'Right,' said Sophie, glancing at Imogen.

'Silly joke,' I muttered. 'Very silly.'

'But you're cute.' She looked at me so directly that the paper frog in my hands bounced out of my agitated grasp on to the floor. Imogen picked it up and handed it to me.

'Thank you,' I said. 'Very nice of you to say so.'

They both laughed and Sophie leaned forward and gave me a hug. I fought desperately against my instinct to stiffen when I am touched without warning. 'You should think about getting some new friends,' she whispered into my scarlet ear. 'Seriously.'

Cook and Freddie were walking towards us, pushing at each other jovially. I relaxed into my seat.

'Our cue to leave,' said Sophie, looking again with distaste at Cook. She winked at me. 'But remember what I said.'

'Right,' I said, feeling as though any moment a camera crew would appear having staged a sadistic TV joke at my expense. I'd probably be seen on the Jonathan Ross show at some point, as part of his warm-up routine. Better to end this now.

'Yes. I will,' I said, giving her a short wave. 'Lovely to meet you, Sophie. Bye.'

Cook and Freddie watched the girls depart.

'Nice arse, that short one,' said Cook coarsely. 'Pity she's frigid. Fucking waste.'

Freddie mouthed 'Jealous' over Cook's head. I smiled nervously.

As I sat practising more origami and the other two joked and bantered and told each to fuck off every so often, I considered my summer so far.

Granted, the blind date had not been a highlight, and neither had my dismal casting as shag referee, but sitting at that table, concentrating on the perfect paper Spitfire, I felt a glow of something very close to happiness. Two girls, who appeared to be in possession of all their faculties, and who more importantly were both at least a number eight on the fit-ometer, had actually preferred me to my cock-of-the-walk best friends.

I was almost tempted to have a celebratory cider. But I resisted.

'Look at Hugh fucking Hefner here,' said Cook, lightly slapping me around the head. 'Who fucking knew, eh Fred?'

Freddie grinned at me and raised his bottle. 'Nice one, JJ,' he said, winking. 'Nice one.'

Effy

Tuesday 25 August

Via San Angelo

'No . . . I've called her niece,' Mum was saying on the phone. 'She wants her buried in England . . .' There was a pause. 'I understand that, but . . . Yes. I know there's paperwork to take care of . . . Right.' She sighed so heavily I could hear it through the wall. 'Yes. Yes. I'll do what I can.'

There was silence, then a frustrated 'Fucking Italian bureaucrats' muttered loudly in the kitchen. She must have ended the call.

I was in my room, sitting up against the door, my legs tucked into my chest, smoking. I coughed, wheezing a bit. I'd been practically chain-smoking since it happened. I felt heavy-headed, rough. I dropped the cigarette into an empty bottle of beer, staring at it as it fizzed and died in the gassy dregs.

I wrapped my arms around me, feeling my ribs. I hadn't eaten anything yesterday, or today. Couldn't. I felt constantly sick. At least the tears were drying up now, gradually being replaced by numbness again. I didn't know which was worse, but at least it'd give my skin a break. The few times I'd looked at my face in the mirror a damp, puffy reflection had gaped back at me. No make-up. Piggy-eyes.

I opened my mouth and said 'Ha', testing that I could still speak.

She and I hadn't spoken since the incident in the kitchen. She hadn't pushed it; just left me, knowing I would only attempt to kill her if she addressed me before I was ready.

Ready to what? Forgive her?

And him. He was nowhere to be fucking seen. I fed myself another little morsel of pain, remembering before. Back when I had thought, I'd actually fucking thought he felt the same as I did. Fascinated, bewitched. Alive.

Had I made it up? Or imagined it?

I got to my feet, went to the cupboard to get a towel and clean clothes and underwear. Then I opened the door and crept to the end of the hall and the bathroom. As I carefully shut the door I watched warily for her appearance out of the kitchen. Nothing, just a waft of smoke snaking out of the door, clouding up.

I ran the bath as hot as I could get it, then stepped in, enjoying the scalding water on my legs, watching them grow pink with alarm. Yesterday evening I'd stayed in the bath for hours, wincing at the boiling water on my shredded knees, just letting the pain flood through me. I lay there until my skin puckered like an uncracked walnut. The water protected me. I lay back now, and pressed my hands to my face, watching the steam clouding up the mirror.

Afterwards I got dressed in my ripped black jeans and Sid and Nancy T-shirt. Then I carefully put on mascara and eyeliner, watching my eyes grow big and smoky. I rubbed moisturiser into my skin, looking at the freckles on my nose – the one remnant of the child Effy. A child no more, that's for fucking sure.

I brushed my wet hair, and sat on the side of the bath running my fingers through it. I picked up the damp towel and shoved it on top of the others. Then I opened the door.

She was standing right in front of me. Her hair was pulled back in an untidy ponytail and her face looked shadowy and tired.

'Hey,' she said carefully. 'Nice bath?'

I nodded, keeping my lips closed. 'Is there any tea?' I said, startling myself with the sound of my voice. 'I really want a cup of tea.'

Her eyes lifted hopefully. 'Course,' she said. 'I'd like some too.'

I sat in the kitchen with my hands in my lap. It was the way I used to sit when I was a kid, after I'd got upset, or Tony had tried to beat me up or something. Mum would just move around the kitchen, making me things: hot chocolate, a boiled egg . . . silently comforting me.

She put a mug of tea in front of me. And then a sandwich. She'd found the only soft white bread in the whole of Italy apparently. It was ham, cheese and pickled onion. My favourite. I swallowed, not wanting to acknowledge this gesture but feeling it in the backs of my eyes.

Mum sat down with her mug, and put her glasses on to read through an official-looking document. I chewed, watching her attempt to make sense of it.

'Is that about Florence?' I said at last.

She looked up and sighed. 'I think so . . . Not that I can understand a bloody word of it.' She gave a short little laugh. 'I should never have agreed to it when Florence told me she wanted me to sort all this out.' She took her glasses off. 'I suppose I didn't think she'd actually die.'

'I miss her,' I said. 'Even though we didn't really know her for long.' I picked up the other half of my sandwich. 'She's just one of those people, you know?'

Mum smiled. 'Yes,' she said. 'She was.'

She watched me as I ate.

'Effy,' she began. 'We need to talk—'

'Don't want to,' I said quickly, my fingers pressing into the sandwich. 'I can't.'

'OK.' She took a slug of tea. 'But it might help.'

'Help who?' I put the food down.

'Both of us.'

'Why should I give a toss if it helps you?' I said calmly. 'Talk to him. I'm sure he's been a tower of strength.'

'We both feel terrible.'

'Oh you should have said earlier.' I smiled nastily. 'Because that makes all the fucking difference.'

'Alfredo thinks you're wonderful,' Mum went on, nervously. 'He feels he . . . may have confused you . . . spending so much time with you.' She swallowed. 'He genuinely wanted to. But not . . . I mean, he's old enough to be your dad. He didn't imagine you would misinterpret his interest.'

'He rubbed his cock against my arse, Mother,' I told her,

227

watching her face for a response. 'He got a fucking hard-on just looking at me.' I pushed the plate away from me. 'I'd say that's pretty fucking difficult to "misinterpret", wouldn't you?'

She stared at me, careful not to betray any sign of hurt. I know that look, because it's one I use regularly myself. The apple doesn't fall far from the tree, as it were.

'He's a man, whose response to a beautiful girl wiggling her bottom around in front of him is going to be a bloody hard-on.'

She was getting riled. Good. I was sick of Saint fucking Anthea.

'Does he do that with your saggy old arse?' I asked breezily. 'Or does he need, like, Viagra to get it up?'

She slammed her palm down on the table. 'Sometimes,' she said, anger vibrating through her, 'you make me fucking ashamed of you.'

'Maybe,' I nodded. 'But you could never in a million fucking years, not even if I streaked butt fucking naked in front of Flo's coffin, be more ashamed of me than I am of you . . . You're a neglectful, selfish bitch.' I paused, staring at her. 'And if you think that's just my opinion, go and ask Dad what he thinks.'

She dropped her head down, giving me a good view of her black roots, specked with grey, obviously.

'I didn't want to hurt your dad. It just happened,' she sniffed.

'You know what?' I said. 'Once I thought that I could trust you. I thought you would fucking look after me, notice stuff that was happening with me.' I rocked slightly against the back of my chair. 'But you never could do that. You've always been so fucking wrapped in your own, self-induced shit.'

'That's not fair.'

'No. No.' I held up my hand referee-style. 'It's totally fucking fair.' I got up now, and leaned back against the fridge. 'But he talked to me. He made me feel like what I said and thought mattered.'

'Your dad?' she said, confused.

I looked at her disdainfully. 'Aldo.'

'Right.' She sighed, getting a tissue out of her jeans pocket. 'Well. I told you, he liked you.'

'But he liked you more, didn't he?' I said. 'For some reason he preferred your whining fucking company to mine in the end.' I shook my head. 'He made sure I good and trusted him. And then he let me down.'

'You can still trust him,' she said. 'And me.'

I snorted. 'You're having a fucking laugh, aren't you Mother?' I gaped at her. 'Me, trust either of you bastards ever again? I don't fucking think so.'

There was silence. Mum took a cigarette from her packet and lit it. She blew out some smoke and looked at me.

'Sit down, Effy.'

'I don't want to sit down.'

'Please. Just for a minute.'

Reluctantly I dragged out a chair to some distance from the table and sat on it, agitated.

'I'm sorry,' she said quietly. 'You're right. I have neglected you. I was too busy with my own stuff . . .' She tapped her fag into the ashtray. 'I was very depressed. I couldn't see anything beyond me.'

229

'I noticed,' I said sulkily.

She ignored my tone. 'I knew I'd fucked things up with your dad. It felt like the world had caved in on me. I couldn't see you.' She paused. 'Or what was happening with those boys.'

I said nothing, waiting for her to go on.

'When we got here I felt so fucking old, and washed up. You wouldn't talk to me, didn't want to be with me. I was lonely.'

'Hmmm.' I fiddled with a rip in my jeans. 'Well, you did—'

'Yes, I know. I had an affair. I caused all the grief.' She finished her fag and stubbed it out. 'But your dad's not entirely bloody blameless, you know.'

'No.' I stared down at my lap, thinking of what I'd done to Freddie, and to Cook. I'd played them off against each other. I'd made my own shit, too. Was I any better than Mum? I winced. Maybe this was like karma or something. Getting what I deserved.

'I was an idiot,' I said finally. 'I wanted someone to notice me. Not just for my face or my body, but for me . . . And he did. It was all I needed . . .'

'But Aldo thinks you're great. Really,' she said. 'I was jealous of that at first.'

'Yeah?'

'Yeah. But then he and I . . . we just started talking about . . . marriage and divorce, and failure . . . and all that shit. He understood.' She took out another fag. 'Gradually I began to feel less like fucking Medusa . . . like I could be happy again.'

I stared at a point on the floor.

'Effy, you're young, you're drop-dead bloody gorgeous.

You're clever. You've got all the time in the world to meet and fall in love . . .' She lit her cigarette. 'I haven't got that time. It's not easy watching your beautiful daughter getting all the attention.'

I looked at her, the lines around her eyes, the dark shadows. She had a point.

'How long was it going on?' I asked, bracing myself for the knife in my gut.

'Not long. Nothing happened until Saturday night.' She took another puff. 'We got closer when Florence was taken ill that first time. And it . . . just happened. We realised we both felt the same way.'

'How lovely for you,' I said, but there was no edge in my voice this time. Just resignation.

'In a few months, you'll wonder what the fuck you saw in him,' she said. 'Once you get back to Bristol. To reality.'

'Reality is what I'm afraid of,' I murmured.

'What?'

'Nothing.' I straightened up in my chair. 'Maybe you're right.' I paused. 'So what are we going to do now? Am I going to have to sit around and watch you two getting off with each other?'

'Well.' She regarded me carefully. 'I thought that once I'd sorted out the arrangements with Flo, that you and I could do with a change of scene.' She looked around the kitchen. 'I think we're done with this place.'

'Go back?' I said, not feeling ready for that. Not remotely fucking ready.

'I was thinking of Rome,' she said. 'I've always wanted to go.'

Whatever.

'Not him, though,' I tested. 'He's not coming?'

'No. Just you and me.' She risked a little smile. 'We'll do it properly this time.'

Emily

Wednesday 26 August

The Priory

'Do you want that, or can I have it?' I pointed with my knife at a triangle of cold toast perched on the side of Naomi's plate.

'All yours,' she said, smiling at me as I smothered it in marmalade.

I crammed half of it in my mouth. I was ravenous. The last few days in France I hadn't eaten much. Too excited, and nervous, about coming home.

Naomi clasped her hands together under her chin. 'You eat like a kid,' she said, amused.

'Bloody starving,' I said with my mouth full. I swallowed. 'You not hungry?'

'Not really,' she said. She picked up her latte and sipped it.

'Lovesick,' I said, grinning at her. 'That's what it'll be.'

'Yeah.' She put down her mug and reached across the

table to take my hand. 'That's what it'll be.'

We smiled dopily at each other for a minute, then she let go of my hand.

'So, Em, what shall we do with ourselves today?' she said casually.

I pushed my plate away. 'Go back to yours, spend the rest of the day in your bed, then get up and eat a bountiful dinner, cooked by your mum.'

'I think Kieran's doing the cooking tonight,' she said. 'A celebratory meal.'

'Kieran can cook?' I asked, surprised. 'Doesn't look the type.'

'Yeah, he's a man of mystery is Kieran,' Naomi said in a bored tone. 'I've got a horrible feeling it's going to be a fucking "couples" evening.'

'Aw . . . A double date,' I said, smirking. 'How cosy.'

'How fucking cringe, you mean,' said Naomi. 'Have you spent much time with Kieran, Em?'

'Can't say as I have,' I said. 'I don't normally hang out with crazy politics teachers.'

'Well you're not missing anything.' She spooned out some froth and licked it off her spoon provocatively. 'It's like talking to a slightly monged-out middle-aged socialist with occasional spasms of ADHD.'

'Sounds all right to me,' I said, laughing. 'I mean, I can think of worse things . . . Like dinner round mine, for one.'

'That's true,' she said, dropping the spoon in her empty mug. 'That's an experience I could fucking live without.' She narrowed her eyes, leaning forward. 'Please tell me that will never happen?'

234

I cocked my head to the side. 'Seriously. Can you really imagine my mother cooking us a romantic meal for four?'

'Nope,' said Naomi. 'And that's just the way I want it to stay.'

I sat back in my chair and stretched my arms over my head. I felt full and contented. Naomi and I had settled right back into being together. France . . . Paris . . . seemed like a lifetime ago. I felt a moment's discomfort thinking about Paris, but pushed the thought out of my head. Nothing had happened. It didn't count. I put my arms behind my chair and watched Naomi fiddling with her phone.

'Got a text?' I said, leaning forward.

'Just something from Kieran,' she said, putting the phone face down on the table.

I frowned. 'What about?'

'Oh . . . Just about dinner,' she said vaguely, linking her little finger with mine. 'Nothing important.'

I shut my eyes, letting happiness wash over me. 'You still love me?'

Naomi shrugged. 'S'pose,' she said, sighing.

I pouted, still not totally used to her default dry humour. 'And no one tried to get off with you, right? While I was away.'

'Only Cook,' said Naomi, sniffing. 'And you know he doesn't count.'

'He's unbelievable,' I said, leaning back in my chair. 'He'll literally shag anything that moves.'

'Why thank you, Emily,' she said dryly. 'I'll try not to be hurt by that remark.'

'You know what I mean.' I dragged her arm over towards me. 'He's not safe.'

'I know,' said Naomi, sounding wistful. 'But that's kind of his charm.'

'Whatever,' I said doubtfully. 'I still don't totally trust him. I mean, look what he did to Freddie. Stealing Effy from under his nose.'

'Oh come on,' said Naomi, a bit sharply. 'Little Miss Innocent. Don't make me fucking laugh.'

'Well, it's true,' I said. 'He totally fucking exploited that situation.'

'Right. You mean he forced her to have sex with him? Twisted her fragile little arm till she had no choice?'

'No.' I wasn't going to win this debate, but I carried on just the same. 'I mean he made sure he was in the right place at the right time.' I watched as Naomi shook her head. 'He fucked over his best friend and he took advantage of Effy.'

'Oh boohoo,' said Naomi, getting her purse out of her bag. 'Forgive me if I don't weep tears of pity for Effy Stonem.' She put a five-pound note on the table. 'I mean, don't get me wrong. She's good to hang out with and she's never done me any harm. But I've watched her with those two. She's fucking manipulative.' She zipped up her purse and chucked it in her bag. 'She knows exactly what she's doing.'

I shrugged. 'Maybe.' I got some money out and added it to Naomi's. 'Let's change the subject.'

'Sure,' said Naomi, getting up. 'And decide what we're going to do.'

'How about shopping?' I said. I checked my watch. 'I need an outfit for tonight.'

'You look gorgeous as you are,' said Naomi, looking up and down my cotton playsuit. 'Most fuckable, in fact.'

'But I don't want Kieran to think me fuckable, now do I?' I said coyly.

'Good point,' said Naomi, shuddering. 'The very thought sends me into a tailspin of jealousy.' She grinned at me. 'Though I have a hunch he's into older women at the moment. His brush with student love is well behind him.' She frowned. 'I fucking well hope it is, anyway.'

We paid up and walked hand in hand down towards the shops. Naomi waited till we were round the corner before she grabbed my bum.

'Second thoughts,' she said. 'Do we really need to go to the shops now?' She stroked up to the bottom of my spine. 'It seems such a fucking waste.'

'Just one circuit round Topshop?' I pleaded. 'And then I'm all yours.'

Naomi smacked my bottom a little harder than necessary.

'Ooh, I like Dominatrix Naomi,' I said, wriggling. 'I'll make it a very quick circuit, OK?'

Naomi

Wednesday 26 August

Campbell Dinner

'This looks great,' said Emily, spearing a tube of pasta with her fork. 'What is it again?'

'Rigatoni with radicchio, gorgonzola and a dash of single cream,' announced Kieran, sitting down and tucking his napkin into the neck of his T-shirt. 'You can add a little Speck if you fancy,' he said, picking up his fork. He smiled around the table. 'Dig in.'

Emily and I exchanged a look of suppressed amusement while Mum beamed proudly at Kieran.

'Well,' she said. 'This is nice.' She smiled at Emily. 'We're glad to see you back, Emily. Naomi's been a nightmare the last few weeks.'

'Mum,' I said, scowling. 'Shut up.'

Kieran bounced his fork up and down in the air. 'Seriously,' he said. 'She's not been herself.'

I glared at him, not that he noticed.

Emily looked delighted of course. 'Really?' she said, stirring her food around her plate.

'Yes,' said Kieran, blundering on. 'She's been all over the shop.' He smiled innocently at me. 'Isn't that right?'

I moved my foot subtly under the table and crunched as hard as I could down on his foot. He winced, raising an eyebrow at me.

'You two have no idea how I've been feeling,' I said, looking at him and Mum. 'You've been far too bloody busy—'

'I don't think Emily wants to hear this.' Kieran was blushing. He nudged my foot away from his. 'It'll spoil her appetite.'

There could be no possible argument with that, so we all just sat in silence, apart from the sound of cutlery scraping across plates.

'So,' said Emily after a bit. 'What *has* she been doing?'

I looked at her. 'I told you.'

'Yeah. But I want a second opinion,' she said lightly. 'That's all.'

'Well, she's been helping me a bit in the garden,' began Mum.

Oh, fucking yawn.

'And she's been smoking a lot of the wacky baccy with me,' added Kieran sheepishly.

'And that's about it,' I said quickly, with a pointed look at him. 'Isn't it?'

'Oh,' said Mum, wiping her mouth with her napkin. 'We've talked a bit about next year.' She stopped to drink some beer. 'You know, university and stuff.'

'Yeah?' said Emily. She turned and pinned me down with those bloody doe eyes.

'Not really,' I shrugged, my eyes narrowing. 'Nothing concrete.'

'Well, there was the—' Kieran began.

'Nothing,' I said. I got up with my half-eaten meal. 'Phew, I'm stuffed.' I looked over at Emily who'd eaten everything on her plate. 'We're off to my room now, OK Mum?'

Mum looked at me suspiciously. 'No,' she said. 'It's not OK.' She glanced at Kieran. 'Kieran's gone to a lot of trouble with the dessert.'

'Right.'

I left my plate on the counter and sat back down. I was probably scowling. I felt distinctly fucking irritated with the lot of them.

Kieran disappeared and came back with a vat of Tiramisu.

'I thought you'd probably had your fill of French cuisine,' he told Emily. 'So I plumped for an Italian theme tonight.'

'Great,' said Emily, as he helped her to a huge portion. 'I love Tiramisu.'

'None for me,' I said ungratefully, wrinkling my nose. 'Not keen.'

'Naomi,' said Mum sharply. 'You're being very rude.'

'Sorry!' I threw my hands up in the air. 'But no one fucking asked me if I liked it. And I don't.'

Emily looked well uncomfortable. 'Well, I'll eat your helping,' she said.

Creep.

Kieran smiled at her, pleased.

'Nice to know I have a small, select appreciation society,' he said pleasantly. 'Of two.'

Emily giggled.

'So,' she asked Kieran after a few minutes. 'You've been helping Naomi decide on her future career, then?'

'Well,' he said. 'I've just pointed a few things out, that's all.' He finished off his pudding. 'Naomi wouldn't really take advice from an old crock like me.'

'Too right,' I muttered, willing both Kieran and my mum to fucking disappear.

'OK, Naomi,' said Mum calmly. 'I think you've made your point.' She patted Kieran's hand. 'Shall we clear the table?'

They got up and went into the kitchen laden with bowls.

'Naomi,' hissed Emily. 'What the fuck's up with you?'

'Nothing,' I said sulkily. 'It's just the boring small talk, you know.'

'I didn't think it was boring,' she said, frowning. 'I was interested.'

I pulled her up off the chair. 'Let's go to bed,' I said, kissing the side of her head. 'All I'm interested in tonight is getting you naked.'

Emily smiled. 'Well if you put it like that,' she said. 'I'll skip the coffee and liqueurs. Just for you.'

'We're going upstairs now,' I called out to Mum. 'Play some music and stuff.'

'And the rest,' whispered Emily as I pushed her out of the room. 'Night Gina. Night Kieran.'

An hour later I lay wide awake while Emily slept beside me.

I had to get my act together and make some decisions. I just had to find a way to tell Emily about them.

I looked down at her face, sweet, lips slightly parted, peaceful.

And I wasn't looking forward to that.

Everyone

Thursday 27 August

Uncle Keith's pub quiz

Katie

'Hey Freddie.'

He turned around as I spoke, knocking three full pint glasses with his elbow. He scrabbled to stop them falling off the bar.

'Katie. Hi . . . You OK?'

'Yeah.' I smiled at him. 'I'm OK.' I watched his eyes darting about nervously. 'Really.'

He smiled. 'Good,' he said, hitching up his jeans and blushing. 'I don't want us to—'

I stopped him. 'Just forget it, Freddie,' I said, evenly. 'I'm over it.' I reached into my bag to get my purse. 'It's all good.'

He quickly dug his hand into his pocket. 'Let me get you

a drink,' he gabbled. 'What do you want?'

'It's fine, I'll get my own,' I said, not looking at him. 'But thanks.'

I ordered a Bacardi and Coke, then took a deep breath before carrying it over to where everyone was sitting. Emily, Naomi, Thomas and Pandora, Cook, JJ . . . It was good to see them. It seemed like years, not just weeks.

'Babelicious!' said Cook loudly, grinning at me, obviously already pissed. 'Come and join the love-in.'

I sat in the only available seat. Next to Naomi. I glanced at Emily, who smiled encouragingly at me. Oh well, in for a penny, in for a pound.

I wedged myself into the seat and put my drink on the table. 'Hi,' I said to Naomi, aiming for friendly. 'Mind if I sit here?'

For a second the famous lip-curl threatened her mouth, but stopped just in time. 'Free country,' she said, giving me a half smile.

I returned it and swung back to watch the others.

Cook beamed around the table. 'Couldn't keep away for long, eh?' he said. 'It's the lure of the Cookie Monster, see. None of you fuckers can be without me.'

''Cept for Effy. She ain't here,' said Pandora. She had her chair about as close to Thomas's as it was possible to get without actually sitting on his knee.

'Good point,' said Cook, bowing at her. 'But who fucking cares.' He waved his pint around. 'I'll even fucking drink to it.'

There were a few uncomfortable looks. Freddie studied the door.

'Anyway, Cook,' said Naomi, changing the subject. 'Haven't you got us a little something?'

'Yeah. Right, Princess.' He leant back on his seat and bellowed, 'Oi Keith, where's me fucking drugs?'

Keith, belly bursting out of his stained shirt, looked up from where he was messing about with a microphone by the bar. 'Keep your fucking voice down, Jimbo,' he hissed. He looked furtively around the pub. 'Here.'

A small plastic bag flew across the room, caught neatly by Cook.

'Discreet, isn't he?' Naomi rolled her eyes. 'Your uncle.'

Cook didn't answer, too busy turning the bag upside down. He shook the booty out on the table. 'Help yourselves, children,' he said. 'There's one for anyone who isn't on the mental pills . . . That means you, JJ.'

'Thanks for the reminder,' said JJ, sipping his Coke, but he smiled unbothered at the rest of us.

I took one of the little round pills and swallowed it with a swig of Bacardi.

'What are these, anyway?' I said.

' "E" of course,' said Emily. 'What did you think?'

'Paracetamol?' I suggested, straight-faced.

While Emily gave me the finger, I caught sight of Naomi smiling at us. I wriggled in my seat, feeling the warmth of the alcohol doing its work. I was just beginning to feel relaxed when a sudden ear-piercing screech of feedback made everyone recoil.

'Right you silly cunts,' boomed Keith, using a microphone despite the fact the place was half-empty. He cleared his throat. 'Welcome to Keith's quiz night.' He shuffled some paper in front of him. 'Now, for the fuckwits amongst us, this is how it works.' He paused for dramatic effect. 'You lot divide into teams. I read out the questions, you write down your answers. Winning team get up to three free half-pints of the beverage of my choice.' He cleared his throat again. We all sat passively waiting.

'OK,' he said finally. 'Question Number One . . . Fucus is a type of what?'

'What the fuck is fuckus?' said Freddie, snorting with laughter.

'It's Latin innit, for the act of shagorious,' said Cook, grinning and banging the table. He turned to Pandora. 'Ain't that right, Princess?'

Thomas stiffened, and Panda put a protective arm through his.

'No way,' she said, glaring at Cook. She cuddled up to Thomas, who was trying to rise above it.

'Actually,' said JJ quietly. 'It's pronounced *few-cus*.' He paused. 'And it's a type of seaweed.'

'Nice one, Mastermind,' said Freddie, grabbing a bit of paper and writing it down. 'Just keep it on the low, yeah. We don't want to give our answers away, do we?'

He kissed JJ on the side of his head. JJ smiled, chuffed. We were all looking at him, thankful for his existence. And not just because of his brain.

I leaned in towards Naomi, nudging her gently with my shoulder. 'By the way, I am officially giving my blessing,' I said lightly. 'But just so you know, if you hurt Emily, you're fucking dead.' I smiled and clinked my glass against hers.

'Noted,' said Naomi, raising an eyebrow.

Emily looked over at us. She beamed at me. 'Cheers,' she mouthed.

I waved my hand dismissively and craned over to see what was coming next.

A second burst of feedback split the air, shorter this time.

'Question Number Fucking Two,' said Keith, trying to juggle his question sheet, the microphone and a pint of ale or bitter or whatever it is that disgusting old men drink. 'What is *monophobia*?'

'Is that, like, a fear of wanking?' said Cook, deadly serious. Everyone groaned.

'I know this one,' said Thomas. He looked soppily at Pandora. 'It is the fear of being alone.'

Panda kissed him on the nose while another groan went round the table. I saw Emily rest her head on Naomi's shoulder. Freddie swilled his beer around in his glass, avoiding any eye contact.

Cook was concentrating on shredding a beer mat. 'Bollocks to that,' he said, absently. He looked up, caught my eye. 'Nothing to fear except fear itself, eh Katiekins?' he grinned.

I raised my glass. I'll drink to that.

Naomi

I looked at Emily, eyes shining with happiness. I had to tell her. But how to play it?

'I love you, Emily,' I said.

She beamed at me, 'I love you too. Always.'

I chewed my lip, feigning concentration. 'There's something I keep forgetting to tell you—'

But Em wasn't listening. She'd turned to Freddie.

'Look lively, everyone,' he said. 'Here comes the next one.'

Freds was getting well into writing down the answers. Typical fucking boys.

'Ready, twats?' shouted Keith. 'Question Number Three is one for the ladies.'

He cleared his throat and hocked a load of phlegm into his empty pint glass. There was a collective 'Eww' from all females present. Keith looked totally unbothered.

'Which American rap artiste invited you to lick his lollipop?' He leered around the room. 'Extra points for a practical demonstration on my good self.'

'Fuck, I'd rather bathe in acid,' I muttered.

'Yeah! Ugh, that is well horrible,' added Pandora.

Thomas shook his head in wonderment. 'My mind is now boggling.'

I looked over at Cook, who was cackling and snapping his hand in the air in a ridiculous hip hop style.

'What's so fucking funny? The man's repulsive.' I wrinkled my nose at him. 'No offence.'

'None taken, Princess,' he said, tears of mirth in his eyes. 'But you're wrong. He's fucking brilliant. I love 'im, man.'

No one else seemed to share his opinion. The rest of us were actually concentrating on the question.

'What's the answer, then?' asked JJ, looking impatient.

Freddie widened his eyes comically. 'Fuck's sake, Jay,' he

said. 'You know the name of some fucking obscure type of seaweed, but you've never heard of 50 Cent?'

'Of course I've heard of him,' said JJ loftily. 'I just didn't recognise the lyric.'

'You know, it's the one where he says his willy's like a sweet shop or something,' said Pandora, and she started shrugging her shoulders and rapping. She was fucking monged. That girl cannot handle drugs. Everyone laughed, even Thomas. She looked mental, her eyes closed and a blissful smile on her face.

'So . . .' Cook interrupted, before pausing to burp extravagantly, banging his chest with his fist. 'Which of you ladies is going to wrap their lovely lips around Keith's throbbing member?'

'Oh God, I'm going to be sick,' groaned Katie, making retching noises.

Cook pointed a slightly drooping finger at her. 'Well actually Katiekins, it's got to be you, 'cause Panda's with Thommo and Emily and Naomi here don't do cock.'

'I'm bloody relieved to say,' Emily muttered, snuggling into my chest.

I shifted uncomfortably. 'Shut the fuck up, Cook,' I said. 'There's a good boy.'

'Shut up yourself, dyke,' said Cook, mildly.

I shot him a sharp look, but he had JJ in a headlock, knuckling his head in that fucking homoerotic way of his. While Em had been in France, I felt like I'd bonded a bit with Cook – as much as a lesbian can bond with a savagely heterosexual maniac anyway. But now that Emily was back, the banter had reverted to the old homophobic bullshit.

And I'd got softer again. She has that effect on me. I looked down at her head, nuzzled against me, and stroked her hair off her face.

Emily sat up. 'Anyway,' she said, looking up at me. 'What were you about to tell me? Earlier?'

'Oh. Yeah, that. It's just—'

'Question Number Fucking Four,' bellowed Keith. He paused and looked down at his sheet, perturbed. 'How many pairs of chromosomes, whatever the fuck *they* are, does a human have?'

Freddie threw his pen down. 'Fuck knows.'

'Forty-six,' said Thomas, quickly.

'It's twenty-three, actually,' said JJ, looking pleased with himself. 'He said *pairs* of chromosomes.'

Thomas shrugged. 'A matter of semantics. Humans do have forty-six chromosomes.'

'Don't worry, babe,' said Pandora, stroking his hair. 'I think you're well bloody clever.'

'Well, we were both right, in a sense,' said JJ, magnanimously.

Cook looked bored, while Freddie scribbled down '23' on his answer sheet.

'Yeah, we'd have no chance of winning if it wasn't for you two,' Freddie said, pleased.

Cook rocked back on his chair, his hands behind his head, and produced one of his empty grins. 'I don't give a fuck about winning no stupid fucking quiz. Or a bunch of fucking chromosomes neither. Don't need to know that shit.'

'That's right, Cookie,' I said airily. 'Good thing there's a degree in Pissing Your Life Up the Wall.' I slapped my forehead. 'Oh, no. Sorry. There isn't.'

Emily laughed. The others looked nervous.

'Fucking hilarious,' said Cook, his eyes narrowing. 'And yous two will be down for Carpet Munching Studies, yeah? Clit-flicking 101? Or maybe a BA Honours in being a Stuck Up Bitch?'

Right, I'd had enough of this.

'Yes Cookie,' I snapped. 'I'm going to an open day for Yale on Saturday . . . Because I want more out of life than flipping burgers or whatever fucking soul-destroying dead-end job you're heading for.'

There was a silence, in which I realised with a sinking heart what I'd just said out loud.

Cook raised his eyebrows. 'Is that right, Naomi?' He nodded towards Emily, who was staring wide-eyed at me, confusion and hurt etched on her face. 'Maybe you should have told your girlfriend that first.'

Bollocks.

Emily

'Cheers Naomi,' I hissed as everyone got on with pissing about. 'Thanks a fucking bunch.' I hugged myself. 'You could have told me that before you blabbed it to the pub. Slightly less humiliating, you know.'

'Honey.' She took my hand and held it between both of hers. 'It's no big deal. I still want to be with you, Em.'

251

Her tone was light, but I could tell she felt guilty. It was in her eyes, not quite meeting mine head on.

'You had loads of opportunities to mention it,' I said, my chin wobbling. 'While I was making plans about the gap year for starters.'

I sat back, upset. Don't fucking cry, I told myself. Not in front of everyone. I looked miserably around the table. Thomas and JJ were having a general knowledge willy-waving contest, arguing about Freud. Cook and Freddie were bantering, Katie was fiddling with her phone. Only Pandora was watching us. She caught my eye and smiled in some kind of understanding. Did she understand? She and Thomas looked well loved-up to me. I guess you can never tell what's going on underneath.

Naomi squeezed my hand. 'C'mon babe, don't be like this. I'm just thinking about my future, that's all.'

'What about me, aren't I part of your future?'

I could hear the whine in my voice, and I hated it. But I couldn't help it. I was gutted. And scared.

'Of course you are!' said Naomi. 'It's just a fucking open day.'

I started digging my nail into the wooden table top and gouging out splinters.

'But you'd have to go to America,' I said, sullenly. 'I thought we'd apply to the same uni.'

Naomi sighed, exasperated. 'Come on, Em, that's not realistic. You should go to whatever uni you want to. We're strong enough, aren't we?'

'I just want us to be together,' I said. 'That's the most important thing for me . . . Maybe it isn't for you.'

Naomi said nothing, just trained those ice blue eyes on me, and my heart sank.

'Your silence speaks fucking volumes, Naomi,' I said, my voice breaking.

'OK Emily,' she said, dragging her hand through her hair. 'If you really don't want me to go to the bloody open day, I won't go.'

This was the part where I was supposed to tell her no, she must go. But I couldn't. The relief was too much. I brought Naomi's hand to my lips and kissed it, then rested my head on her shoulder.

'You don't want to go to America anyway,' I said. 'Death penalty and all that. Not good for a girl with a conscience.'

Naomi picked up her drink. 'Yeah. You're probably right.'

'You won't regret it, lover,' I said, kissing her quickly on the cheek. 'I promise.'

Cook

'QUESTION NUMBER FUCKING FIVE.'

Here we go again. I was sick of the poxy quiz. It wasn't doing nothing for my self-esteem. I know fuck all, about anything.

Keith lurched against the bar, drunk as a fucking skunk. 'Who said "I wouldn't recommend sex, drugs or insanity for everyone, but they've always worked for me"?' He looked around the room and did a volcanic fucking burp.

'That's easy,' said Naomi, fiddling with her hair.

'Give the rest of us a fuckin' chance,' I said, balancing seven shot glasses of absinthe in my hands. Time for Cookie to get this fucking party started.

'What is it?' asked Freddie, looking suspiciously at the drinks.

'Calm down, Gaylord,' I said, plonking the shots down on the table. 'Keep your fucking wig on. It's *absinthe*.' I downed mine immediately. 'Tequila weren't hitting the mark.'

Panda picked one up and held it to the light. 'Wow, look at that,' she said, seriously fucking pilled. 'It's flipping beautiful. All green like a . . . like a beautiful emerald sea.'

'You know what absinthe is, Panda?' said Thomas, gawping at it with her. 'It is aniseed spirit.'

'Clever,' said Panda, giving him a kiss on the cheek.

'All right,' I said, 'Enough of this soppy bollocks.' I ruffled Thomas's hair. 'You want to watch out, mate. She's turning you into a right fucking pussy.'

Thomas didn't react. Still some shit going down there, obviously.

I caught Freddie's eye. He was sniffing into his glass like a girl.

'Having a good time?' I asked.

'Yeah,' he said. 'Course.'

'You wanna tell your face, mate.' I laughed. 'You look like someone's fucking died.'

'Shut up, Cook,' Freddie said quietly. 'I'm not in the mood, all right?' He nodded at Naomi. 'So,' he asked, pen poised over paper. 'What's the answer?'

'It's—'

'I'm sure I know this one,' JJ leapt in, worried he'd get his fucking boffin crown nicked.

'Well, I *know* I know it,' said Naomi, nose stuck in the air.

She was totally getting on my tits tonight. It's like since her girlfriend came home she's fucking lost her sense of humour. Me and her, we were getting on all right before. I'd never tell a fucking soul, but for once I quite liked hanging out with a girl and not shagging her.

'Well what the fuck is it, then?' I said. 'Spit it out.' I grinned at her. 'Though, obviously that would be a novelty for you.'

She flared her nostrils at me. 'Hunter S. Thompson,' she said.

'Oh, of course,' said JJ.

'Right because you're into all them psychedelic druggy books, eh, Jay?' I said. 'You're so fucking "out there" yeah?'

Everyone went silent.

JJ shrugged. 'The two are not mutually exclusive,' he said. 'Reading about drugs, and not taking drugs. Well—' he paused. 'Not recreational drugs.'

'Didn't understand a fucking word of what you just said, mate.' I sniffed. 'I need a fucking dictionary to converse with my friends these days.'

JJ looked down at his hands.

'Stop being a wanker, Cook,' said Freddie. 'Don't take it out on JJ.'

'What the fuck are you talking about?'

'It's just a fucking pub quiz,' Fred went on. 'I don't know any of the answers either.' He nodded at me. 'Seriously. Calm down. It'll be all right, mate.'

The others looked at us, wondering what the fuck was going on.

'Will it, Fred?' I asked him, downing a couple more shots. 'Can you promise me that?'

Keith was revving up for the next question. Feedback pierced the atmosphere.

'Ah fuck it,' I said, grinning at everyone. 'Each to their own.' I winked at Naomi. 'Eh, Princess.'

'Right Cook,' she said. 'Now go and get us all a proper fucking drink.'

Freddie

While Cook worked himself up into a lather about being thick, doing his best to get annihilated, I looked over at Katie. She was cramming crisps into her mouth and chatting with Naomi. Something had to have happened over the past month, 'cause neither of these things are normal on Planet Katie.

When Emily got up to go to the loo I moved over to her seat.

'Just for a minute,' I said, as Katie's mouth opened. 'OK?'

She finished her crisps. 'Don't tell me you want to have a conversation with me?'

'Why not?' I said. 'We used to be friends, didn't we?'

She smiled. 'Yeah, we did.'

'So,' I began, casually. 'What have you been doing with yourself lately?'

'This and that,' said Katie, licking salt off her fingers. 'Went to France, had a massive fight with Emily in Paris, then . . .' she paused. 'Then I went to Venice.'

My heart stopped. 'You saw Effy?'

'Yeah,' said Katie, watching me carefully. 'It was a bit weird.'

'But you—'

'Yeah, I know. I wanted to clear the air, I suppose.'

'Right,' I said. 'Did you?'

'Not really,' she said. 'Same old in the end.' She paused. 'But in a way, it made me feel better about stuff, being with her, watching her.' She bit her lip. 'She's still messed up about what happened.'

I looked down. 'Right.' Fuck, now it was going to start all over again.

'She seeing anyone else?' I blurted out.

A vision of Effy on the back of some bastard's fucking Vespa flashed into my head. Why did I ask? I didn't want to fucking know.

Katie hesitated. 'No,' she said. 'No, she isn't. Wasn't.'

I nodded, trying not to show relief. Not that it fucking mattered.

'QUESTION NUMBER FUCKING SIX.' Keith was sitting down now, red-eyed and sweating. 'And it's a language one.' He cleared his throat. 'To the nearest five years, when was the word CUNT first heard on British TV?' he said. 'That's C.U.N.T. CUNT, as in fanny, twat, minge, cock-holster, beef fucking curtains. And, to quote my favourite comedian, God rest his soul, if you are what you eat, then I'm a cunt.'

He looked around delightedly, waiting for his applause. He didn't get any.

'Ugh. He's got horrid white stains on his trousers,' said Pandora, squinting into the bottom of her glass like if she tried hard enough it would magically refill itself.

Cook was too busy playfully pulling Naomi's hair to notice.

'Piss off, you child,' she said, laughing.

I turned to Katie. 'Is she coming back?' I said. 'Effy?'

Katie shrugged. 'Dunno. Have to wait and see I suppose.'

We exchanged a mutually apprehensive smile.

'Right, then,' I said, focusing on the question and waving my pencil around. What's the answer?'

Thomas pulled at his bottom lip. 'It will have been quite recently, I think.'

'1970,' said Cook out of the blue. He belched casually.

'Sure about that?' said Naomi.

'Or thereabouts . . . Gotta be back in them days when people blurted out shit live on TV and no one could fucking stop 'em,' said Cook. 'It's not rocket science, Princess.'

Naomi cuffed him around the ear. 'I'm impressed,' she said. 'There's hope for you after all, Cookie.'

Cook did his best to look as fucking nonchalant as possible, but there was no mistaking he was chuffed. The rest of us smiled.

'Next one, when you're ready, Maestro,' Cook shouted over at Keith, who was about to lose conciousness judging by the way he was slumped over his mic. 'Piece of fucking piss, this.'

'Watch out, JJ,' said Thomas. 'I am feeling good about the next one.' He rubbed his hands together. '*Je suis le feu*, as you say over here.'

I laughed. 'I don't think so, my Congolese *ami*.'

'Where's Keith, anyway?' asked Katie, looking around.

'Fucking hell, the old bastard's passed out,' said Freddie, pointing to a pair of tatty shoes sticking out from behind the bar. 'Cook, sort it out will you?'

Cook ran over and disappeared behind the bar. He jumped up a second later brandishing the question sheet and leaving Keith to potentially choke on his own vomit.

'I've got the answers,' he sang, wafting it through the air. 'What's it fucking worth?'

'Don't be a twat, Cook,' said Freddie. 'Just read the question.'

'Please yourself,' said Cook. He picked up the microphone.

'QUESTION NUMBER FUCKING TEN,' he shouted, mimicking his uncle with impressive accuracy. He held the paper up and read out, 'Which planet is closest to the sun?' Ignoring everyone else in the pub, he looked exclusively over at our table.

Naomi shrugged. 'I don't know anything about astrology.'

Thomas looked pained. 'It is either Mercury or Venus.' He tapped his forehead with his fingers. 'Dammit. I cannot remember,' he said finally, looking annoyed.

I, however, was full of confidence. The intense astrology phase I went through when I was seven was now about to pay off for me.

'Ahem.'

Everyone's eyes turned to me. 'Mercury, of course,' I said, simply.

'Yay, JJ!' said Pandora, clapping her hands. 'I mean, sorry for you Thommo.' She patted his knee.

Thomas's eyes glinted competitively. 'Be careful, JJ,' he said. 'Boastfulness is a shallow trait amongst men.'

'I am not boasting,' I said. 'I simply knew the answer.'

'Yeah,' said Katie. 'It's not a competition, you know.'

We all looked witheringly at her. Even Pandora.

'It's totally a competition,' she said. 'Silly.'

Katie tossed her hair. 'I mean between those two.' She nodded at Thomas and myself. 'The Boffin Brothers.'

'Flattery,' I told her, 'will get you everywhere, Katie.' I sighed. 'I may be facing a lifetime of abstention from the everyday stimulants that the rest of you enjoy,' I said. 'But I will go to my grave a proud man if I carry on excelling at Uncle Keith's fortnightly pub quiz.' I paused. 'Truly, I will.'

'Give us a cuddle, Jay,' said Cook, lumbering towards me. 'I feel the love coming.'

Freddie grinned as Cook clambered around the table to embrace me.

'Please fuck off, Cook,' I said, holding him at arms' length. 'I appreciate your sentiment, obviously, but your breath smells, and I need to go to the toilet.'

Cook nuzzled my head with his. 'Don't ever leave me, will

you mate,' he whispered hoarsely into my ear. 'Promise Cookie you won't ever leave.'

'Promise,' I said carelessly. 'Now get off.'

Effy

Friday 28 August

Italy – somewhere in the sky

'Can I have a glass of red?' said Mum, scanning the wine list. She pointed at the one she wanted. 'That one, please.' She nodded at me. 'Effy?'

'Double vodka please.' I stared at the stewardess. 'Make it cold.'

She smiled tightly. 'I'll see what I can do,' she said, taking the list off Mum.

Mum settled down in her seat. 'Thank Christ we got upgraded,' she said, looking out of the window at the clouds. 'After the past few days I couldn't face bloody Cattle Class.'

From somewhere in Economy came the sound of a baby wailing. We smiled at each other.

Mum took my hand. 'You'll love Rome,' she said. 'It's got a bit more life to it than Venice. More of the bustle. More people.' She closed her eyes.

The stewardess arrived with our drinks. I sipped at mine,

making eye contact with a good-looking scruffy boy sitting down the aisle. I looked away first.

'That place was a bit freaky,' I said finally.

'What, Venice?'

'Yeah. Intense.'

'I know what you mean,' said Mum, taking a gulp of wine. 'Still, it was interesting . . .'

I took another sip of my vodka. I felt fragile. Physically and emotionally.

'I'd have settled for relaxing in the end,' I said, leaning back against the head-rest. 'I think it just made things twice as bad for me.'

Mum looked over at me. 'I'm sorry,' she said. 'I'm really sorry.'

I shrugged. 'It was my fault. I deserved to be punished.'

'Don't be silly,' she said quietly. 'That's not how it works.'

'How does it work, then?' I said. 'I haven't got a fucking clue.'

'Nobody has, babe,' she said. 'You just make it up as you go along, hoping to learn something along the way.'

'Thank you Reverend Stonem,' I said evenly. 'I'll bear that in mind.'

Mum's eyes were closed again, but her mouth twitched.

'You'll be fine, Effy,' she said sleepily. 'Promise.'

I looked across her at the billowing white through the window. Right then, I couldn't imagine it being 'fine' ever again. I couldn't run away for ever, I had to go home, back to them. The thought of Freddie's eyes, flicking away from me in rejection; it was almost paralysing.

When you come between friends like that, you never think

that they'll choose each other over you. I had totally fucking underestimated the bond between Freddie and Cook. Maybe deep down they could never love a girl like me more than they love each other.

And maybe that was the way it should be.

We were staying in Rome for a week or two and then Mum and I were flying home. She'd been honest and told me upfront that she and Aldo were going to be in touch. She'd probably go back to Italy to see him. She wanted me to know, she said. She didn't want secrets any more.

'Secrets,' she said. 'They destroy people's lives.'

Diary of a SNOB

Diary of a SNOB
Poor little Rich Girl
Grace Dent
978 0 340 98974 6 £5.99 PB
OUT NOW!

Diary of a SNOB
Money can't buy me love
Grace Dent
978 0 340 98975 3 £5.99 PB
MAR 2010

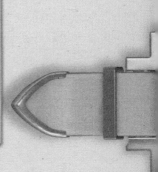

ALSO BY GRACE DENT:
Diary of a Chav

Book 1: TRAINERS V. TIARAS

Book 2: SLINGING THE BLING

Book 3: TOO COOL FOR SCHOOL

Book 4: LOST IN IBIZA

Book 5: FAME AND FORTUNE

Book 6: KEEPING IT REAL

www.bebo.com/poppetmontaguejones
www.shirazbaileywood.co.uk

Also by Sarra Manning

let's get lost

ome girls are born to be bad ... Isabel is one of them. Her iends are terrified of her, her teachers can't get through her... her family doesn't understand her. And that's just e way she likes it. See, when no one can get near you, no one will know what keeps you awake at night, what u're afraid of, what has broken your heart ... But then Isabel meets the enigmatic Smith, who can see right hrough her act. Bit by bit he chips away at her armour, nd though she fights hard to keep hold of her cool, and er secrets, Isabel's falling for him, and coming apart at the seams when she does

Also by Sarra Manning

guitar girl

Seventeen-year-old Molly's band was always just about being a girl, singing Hello Kitty Speedboat and pretending to play instruments with her best mates Jane and Tara. But then the arrogant Dean and his sidekick T hijack the band and suddenly the fluffy girl band becomes *The Hormones* - a real band with a record deal - and they're heading for the big time. Molly slips further and further away from her old life and straight into a tangled love-hate relationship with Dean. Then there are the constant parties, the drugs and the phonies who pretend to like you when they don't ... Molly is living her dream, and she's never felt lonelier in her life. But has she got the strength to walk away from the band, and start again?

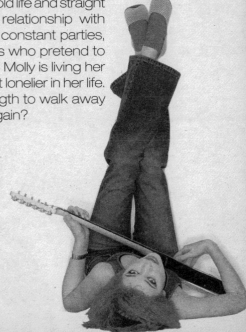

978 0 340 86071 7

Sarra Manning

NOBODY'S GIRL

Bea thinks she's the most boring seventeen-year-old in the world.
She's not pretty or popular or funny, unlike her mother who had Bea
when she was 17. The only glamorous thing about Bea is the French
father who left before she was born and lives in Paris. She yearns for
la vie Parisienne every moment of her dull existence.

So when Ruby Davies, the leader of her school's most elite clique picks
Bea as her new best friend and asks her to go on holiday with them,
she's wary but delighted. If nothing else it's two weeks away from her
over-protective mother. But when the gang arrive in Spain, Bea is
crushed to realise that Ruby and her posse have simply been using her.

978 0 340 88373 0 £5.99 PB
MAR 2010

http://sarramanning.blogspot.com
www.twitter/sarramanning

Vampire Diaries

Vampire Diaries
The Awakening & The Struggle

L. J. SMITH

978 0 340 99914 1 £5.99 PB
OUT NOW!

Vampire Diaries
The Fury & The Reunion

L. J. SMITH

978 0 340 99915 8 £5.99 PB
OUT NOW!

Vampire Diaries
The Return: Nightfall

L. J. SMITH

978 1 4449 0063 7 £5.99 PB
MAR 2010

...g the time of the Italian Renaissance, brothers, Damon a...
... Salvatore fell in love with a beautiful young vampire nam...
...herine. Though Katherine's heart was big enough for both...
...hers, each of them vied to make her his own. The battle fo...
...erine's affection led to her eventually death, and left the tv...
boys immortal, heartbroken, and forever quarreling.

Soon to become a major new ITV series

L. J. SMITH

The *New York Times* Bestselling Author

DARKE ACADEMY

The Darke Academy is a school like no other. An élite establishment that moves to an exotic new city every term, its students are impossibly beautiful, sophisticated and rich. And the more new scholarship girl Cassie Bell learns about the Academy, the more curious she becomes.

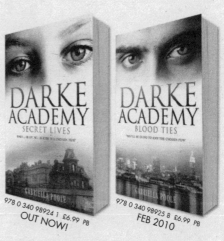

978 0 340 98924 1 £6.99 PB
OUT NOW!

978 0 340 98925 8 £6.99 PB
FEB 2010

GABRIELLA POOLE

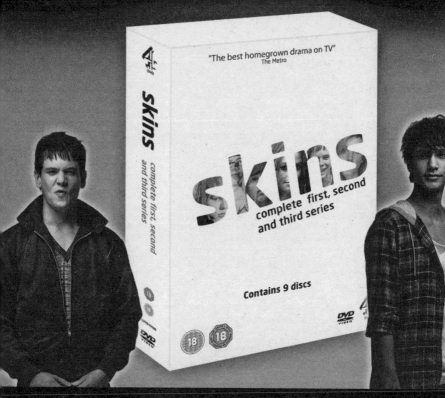